DEMENTIONAL

By Tonya Cannariato

Katarr Kanticles Press

Dementional

By Tonya Cannariato

Katarr Kanticles Press
Texas, USA
Edited by Dionne Lister
Cover Art by Gayla Drummond
Copyright © 2012, Tonya Cannariato
All Rights Reserved.

ISBN-13: 978-0692448236 (Katarr Kanticles Press)
ISBN-10: 0692448233

DEMENTIONAL

Prologue

"I love you." I groan as the tingles advance up my toes and feet, and the characteristic sparkles edge my vision.

I'll never know whether Sarah heard me this time. Or any other time I've told her, for that matter.

My problem is that the dimensional shift can come without me stirring; I'm in the middle of a conversation, and the other person doesn't know I've begun moving in the mysterious sub-atomic spaces.

This time my shift is lucky: the Sarah looking back at me from behind doe-brown eyes looks similar to the one to whom I had just confessed my emotions. Same short brown hair with auburn highlights, same angular cheekbones, though the hollows beneath them are a little more pronounced. This version hasn't been eating well, I can see from the paper-thin texture of her previously fine skin. I'm even still holding her by her shoulders, though her coat is threadbare now.

I know Sarah is suspicious, as I try to regain my footing in the conversation. In every incarnation I've known her, she is quick to catch details out of sync. She is dearer to me every time she notices that I'm not quite the same person she's known.

It's my first mission every time I notice the leaves have changed shape, or the road is made of a different material, or even that the skin on my hand has molted to some new form: Find the Sarah of this reality. I consider myself something like her guardian angel, though that sounds more maudlin than I intend. She is a sort of gravity well for me, and though we've been together in dimensions that can't be explained in human terms, and I couldn't describe the equivalent of what color her eyes were or whether she had hair, her soul chimes at a specific frequency that brings out the best in my own. And lets me know her regardless of the form in which it's cloaked.

This Sarah murmurs something I don't quite catch, and I strain my senses to pick up the thread of her words.

"Never mind."

My silence had dragged on too long. My opportunity has slipped through my fingers.

She eyes me askance and slips swiftly from between my hands, hurrying down what I now see is a dimly lit cobblestone road in a poor neighborhood. It's not one I've seen before, though that's hardly unusual since I began this dimensional shifting.

I'm not too worried about losing track of her now: she ducks into the back door, behind a milliner shop—its sign hanging by rusty chains in front of the careworn facade. The shop window only houses one modest hat in its display rack, and I worry at this further evidence of Sarah's financial straits.

I wish there were some way to show her that my apparent unreliability is actually a working partnership.

Chapter 1

I started this adventure as a research scientist, carrying on where the Montauk experiments seemed to have failed; deep in the bowels of a remote naval station. The government didn't want to risk civilian exposure a second time, given the proliferation of ghost stories, sightings, and conspiracy theories after that early experiment.

Even the Large Hadron Collider was deemed too public for this kind of research, so, with typical efficiency, some bureaucrat chose a random mountain in the Denali chain. My whole department got shifted to the 63rd latitude—after a few years of bickering and building. In the meantime, my research showed great promise. Focusing multiple lasers on a single point could give us access to alternate dimensions. We were now able to strengthen our defensive capacity without resorting to more offense. That was the theory, anyway.

I was happy enough to be doing something in line with my pacifist inclinations, though it was a lot to ask of Sarah to move out to the wilds of Alaska—even if we were within 100 miles of Anchorage, which had a population of a third of a million people. She took the request in stride, though, and decided her creative self would be satisfied by learning local crafts from the native population.

Life was good—or at least on something of a normal/expected track. I was young enough that when I asked her to marry me, I was all nerves and thumbs, but being on a government payroll and housed within government apartments, I had the extra cash to be able to be extravagant with my proposal. I felt lucky when she said yes.

It wasn't long after her commitment, though, that my life started feeling like it was the storyline for a *Twilight Zone* episode. At first, I put down the missing papers and unexpected experiment results to distractions related to our wedding planning, but even Sarah started noticing a change in the atmosphere in the housing complex.

In hindsight, I suppose we were gullible to assume my superiors would resolve the situation—or even that it would be possible to close the Pandora's Box we had opened with our early tests. But I was trained as a scientist, and had supreme faith in the scientific method. I still wonder if the team had had more people of faith—or even just naïveté—whether I would be on this dark path.

Richards, my boss, while always a methodical and brilliant man, was careful to keep us younger set away from anything that smacked of spirit—let alone a collaborative *esprit de corps*. His answer to everything was competition and more layers of secrecy. I don't think I know what any of the other members of the team were experimenting with in the same lab, let alone in the same complex. Maybe there were quantum entanglements we should have taken into account in our calculations. But those thoughts don't help me put my world back together, nor track down the rift I need to plug, to put me back where I belong.

Sarah was worried enough to ask whether we should postpone our nuptials, but I didn't want to wait. She might still change her mind. She was that supportive, loving, once-in-a-lifetime mate for me, and I wanted the world to know it. So on a bright June morning, true to all wedding clichés, we exchanged our vows in a small local church in front of a handful of colleagues and friends. We planned a visit back to the DC area to give our parents, who were older anyway, a chance to show us off. Being only children, we decided to be selfish and keep the main ceremony small and private. Without the weight of extra eyes, I was more comfortable sharing my awe at Sarah's agreement to join her life with mine.

As it turned out, I wish they could have been there, because while the ceremony was beautiful, something about the collection of colleagues assembled started the sub-atomic changes that are pushing me further and further from my birth dimension. I never got a chance to see them once I was wed.

Chapter 2

The flicker of the candles that we lit in memory of absent family members offered a soft glow to the scene. The many, private rehearsals of the vows I'd written to honor Sarah were for naught, as my voice choked on the emotion of sharing them. My hands still shook as we fumbled to place our rings on fingers gone clammy. But when I leaned in for our first married kiss, crushing the roses in Sarah's bouquet between us, the softness of her lips grounded me in reality. Afterward, everyone joined us in the community hall on base to enjoy cake and champagne. Our plan was to escape into the wilderness for a bit of camping in the perpetual light that is an Alaskan summer. Our escape was thwarted when, almost in unity, pagers and cell phones started buzzing and ringing throughout the hall. This was an emergency: all scientists were being summoned to their projects to deal with imminent disaster.

I gave Sarah an apologetic kiss. "Are you sure you're OK waiting up for me? I promise I won't miss our wedding night."

"Go on; if you don't, who knows what might blow up." Sarah had that mischievous sense of humor that wouldn't let her get depressed over cutting short our celebration. I hoped I saw a hint of sadness, anyway.

I was reluctant to leave her behind, even though I knew she didn't have the security clearance to accompany me. As I left the hall, I kept sneaking guilty glances back in her direction, marveling at her grace and beauty. A part of me was keening despair at having to ruin such a momentous day because of work.

As I scanned the readouts on the app I'd created for my iPhone, the nervous butterflies in my stomach left over from the ceremony doubled. My experiment with the Higgs boson was creating some truly spectacular dark matter ripples, and was threatening to break containment. If I didn't hurry, there might not be an apartment to return to.

My steps lengthened as the hall slipped from view; I was running to my assigned lab. Red lights flashed, alarms screamed along the hall-ways, as normally sedentary scientists were suddenly being forced to move quickly in hopes of averting disaster.

I fumbled my security credentials at nearly every checkpoint as a new siren took up the wailing serenade. None of my colleagues were in any better shape: some were so single-minded there were truly spectacular collisions as bodies careened off each other. It would have been humorous if we hadn't all been galvanized by the deadly seriousness of the warnings.

It would only occur to me later how strange it was that all our experiments would hit a crisis point simultaneously. What was so special about June 6, 2012?

Dementional

I used to laugh about the fools who believed the apocalyptic tales predicting the end of the world in 2012, but in my inadvertent adventures in alternate realities, I'm beginning to think every time-line has a moment of crisis—a turning point when that reality's participants are forced to choose whether their space-time implodes or evolves.

Chapter 3

My first indication that things were beyond fixing slapped me in the face, as I finally made it through my lab's steel-reinforced door, which appeared to be melting around the edges. When I turned around to close it against the discordant klaxons ringing in the hall, I noticed it was difficult to reach the handle—as if there were a tangible dark matter impact on my ability to interact with physical material.

Despite the fact that there has never been any lab result that indicates this is a possibility on a macro level, I'm intrigued enough that I play with the field for a few minutes before a strangely distorted sound recalls me to the urgency of the alarm going off in my office. Backing away from the strange door, I next noticed extreme cold radiating from my lab bench. I would have guessed it was heat: the visuals were presenting as liquid mirage waves. The immediate frosting of my breath and eyebrows gave definitive sensory feedback about the arctic temperature.

Looking just beyond the surface to the stainless steel cabinet that normally stored my equipment and experimental tools, I was perplexed. The space I kept locked was warped open.

Everything I had stored was supposed to be inert, so I wasn't even sure where to begin troubleshooting. My first thought was to push through the weird atmospheric resistance and fire up my desktop to access data on projects that should have been dormant. Before I could even get that far, though, I felt the equivalent of a concussive force and the disturbing sensation of unseen fingers plucking at my skin. Heat passed quickly into excruciating pain—it felt like my cells we being torn from my being, one at a time. I blacked out.

Chapter 4

My first hope on waking was that other fail-safes in the compound had kept Sarah safe. My main focus, though, was the nerve memory of unbearable pain. I suspected I had a concussion or broken bones. Nothing looked familiar. Even the colors were wrong for where I thought I should be. I remembered the alarms and being in my lab, trying to head to my office. I wondered whether I had been taken to a new infirmary as a natural follow-on to my lack of responsiveness. I felt around, but couldn't find an edge to a bed, and the surface I was exploring felt more like cement in any case.

I became even more concerned at the eerie silence; during normal operations, there was always the susurration of the air reprocessing fans and the hum of electronics chasing down the latest data point. I didn't even hear footsteps in the hallway. When I knocked against the floor in an increasingly frantic attempt at re-establishing normal perception, I heard a strange kind of thud. This confirmed the blast hasn't rendered me deaf, and I tried clearing my throat.

I felt the rumble of phlegm and heard the rasping noise I normally produce, but felt dissociated from these physical processes.

Raising my hand to my face to scrub at my eyes, it was everything I could do not to shriek in horror: what approached my head from the floor was nothing like the indoor-pasty, white skin on a bony arm that I expected. Instead, I saw scales and claws. I passed out again.

I later understood this to be a dimensional shift—something I had never thought possible. It was a rude awakening, and firmly established that I should suspend any expectation of normal experience.

The next time I awoke in that existence, my subconscious had adjusted, and I was able to come to terms with being some sort of lizard man until I could sort out where my original experiment had gone wrong.

My screaming priority was to find Sarah. Where was she? Had she followed me? I needed to find her.

My second foray at moving my new body was marginally more successful—at least this time I was able to maneuver my new body to stand. I investigated the room, albeit on wobbly legs. I still don't know if my newborn moves were because of the dimensional shift or because my consciousness was not accustomed to handling a body built to such dramatically different specifications than what I remembered of my humanity.

In the end it didn't matter; I allowed my body to propel itself forward of its own accord, and discovered a world strangely similar to what I had left behind—but eerily different. As I made my way out of the lab in which I had woken up, I saw other beasts who matched me. I tried to model my posture after theirs, assuming that I didn't want to draw attention to the anomaly that had brought me to this space-time.

In this version, we also appeared to be scientists testing innovative defenses.

I heard the background noise of conversation, and assumed I was in a large auditorium. Looking around, though, I discovered I was in a hallway, where other small groups were dispersed at a distance. I could feel my heart thud faster; had I lost my mind and had a psychotic break? Strange prickles at the crown of my head forced me to reach up to investigate. I had a frill up there that was standing on end. Inconvenient that my distress was that visible. I leaned against the wall and took a deep breath. A mental inventory assured me I was still able to ask a logical string of questions.

Next task: focus on the babble. What were they saying? I soon discovered a variety of personalities discussing a wide range of scientific content. I decided if crazy was being at a convention where I could tune into whichever content stream most interested me at a given moment, it had its benefits.

As fascinating as this was, I craved my previous reality. I needed to discover where I was, and how to return to my new bride.

Chapter 5

This new form seemed to have a lot of mental storage capacity, and reflected its own life experiences back at me, opening, for the first time (for me, anyway), the question of what constituted soul and what constituted consciousness. Even more intriguing, as I trawled the corridors of this facility, there was a group testing theories that reminded me of some of the psychedelic experimentation in the 60s. I was tempted to offer myself as a subject, hoping that might jolt me out of what was an increasingly unwelcome trip; but decided I didn't have sufficient information to take that risk. After all, I had promised Sarah I wouldn't miss our wedding night—and there was a good chance I had already done exactly that.

I made my way toward the surface of this version of our mountain stronghold cum lab, hoping nobody would find it odd that I was abandoning my experiments in the middle of the afternoon. While sneaking, I had the bad luck to run into this reality's version of Richards. He was saurian like me, and I had to imagine myself with a pointy snout based on looking at his face. It gave me the heebie-jeebies; I had never considered myself particularly vain, but looking at something snakelike, with intelligence peering back at me, pushed all my atavistic fear buttons.

"What are you staring at? Why aren't you in your lab?" The questions rumbled in my direction. How did I know this was Richards? I thought I recognized this being as Richards. What if he wasn't? How did I know he was my boss here too? How did I even comprehend the spitting hisses as a language?

"I need to go check on Sarah." It was a shot in the dark, but he took in my comment with a glint of amusement.

"You've already been married a month. The honeymoon should be over by now!"

I almost hissed at his comment; I hadn't known how the timelines reflected each other. It wasn't a good sign that I had missed my wedding night here.

"Go check on your bride, and take over egg-turning duty on the hatching ground for the rest of the afternoon. I'll cover your lab for you."

This was so unlike the man I had known as Richards; I gawked some more. He chortled and shuffled off sharing the non-verbal thought: "I'm still impressed Sarah managed to produce three viable eggs so soon after your mating."

This was all a bit much to process. I worried I had been leaking information to this stranger, given the back-handed way he shared his thoughts with me, but decided not to dwell on it. The question was: How did I make this body move as fast as I wanted it to go?

Now, any time a solicitous colleague asked as I made my way to the surface, I had a viable excuse. And I learned more about the various forms of communication we all shared. It was still weird to me to hear comments in my head, but it was remarkable how quickly I acclimated to the experience.

The unexpected bonus of this form of communication was that colleagues who had formerly been cyphers in my existence were now open about their own quirks, interests, and needs—and had no problem sharing their images about where I might find my wife. I had a much more complete vision of the sprawling complex than I had ever had in my previous existence, so was able to make my way to an area I otherwise would not have known: the area Richards had named the hatching grounds.

I arrived at the hatching ground to be set upon by a smaller, enthusiastic lizard person. Another snake-like face with a vestigial crest was not what I wanted to see. It startled me so, I held it at arm's length just long enough to figure out I had found Sarah.

She pouted. "I thought you were here to see me?"

"I am. Uh. I just must've still had my head in my project." I wasn't sure I'd ever get accustomed to the scales, but I could remember that my lizard brain thought she was as cute as I remembered my human Sarah.

I hoped the lizard part of me was also right that the hiss she produced meant she was laughing at my thick-headedness.

For all that we wore lizard bodies, we were still mostly upright creatures. I was surprised at how human-like hugs and kisses were in this new form. But greeting Sarah with such familiarity in such an unfamiliar form felt voyeuristic: She both was and wasn't the woman I loved, and I didn't want her to be unfaithful to any version of me. So I broke away from her affectionate greeting rather abruptly. Hurt flashed in her eyes. I couldn't bear that either, so cuddled her close and murmured soothing noises over the top of her head.

That vantage point brought me my first unobstructed view of the hatching grounds. Conveniently enough, given the hollowed-out mountain that served as our base of operations, some intrepid explorer had found a lava tube situated close enough to a sill to be quite warm. There on the rocky ground, were three ivory-colored ovoids, each at least a meter long. Their leathery finish reminded me of tanned hides.

It took a moment of courage to review this me's version of events. It seemed that marriage and mating were rare occurrences here, and thus celebrated throughout the community with a great deal of support. It brought a whole new level of meaning to the expression in my previous world about needing a village to raise a child. Children had been such an abstraction when we had decided to get married in my world. Now they were a fait accompli. And I had missed not only my wedding night but the magic of sharing myself with my new wife to engender life. I was crushed.

As traumatic as the parenthood realization was, it was even worse to know that I (the I that had lived as a human) hadn't created these children, and their mother was now snuggled against some impostor version of myself. It was a strange schizophrenia to be thinking of myself as a stranger, when, by all accounts, I wasn't all that different from what I had been prior to shifting into this dimension. It was my first confrontation with the need to understand the role of spirit or soul within a physical experience, and I didn't have the vocabulary to frame my own confusion in a useful inner debate.

Certainly the holographic universe theory had never personalized the math for me in any way that would lend itself to this kind of experience. And if I were living out a proof of that theory, did the math mean there was some ultimate version of me that was now reflected in this reality? And how many versions of me could there end up being? If I remembered the original postulate, there should only be one reflection of the hologram; but that begged the question of which version of me was the real me? What if both of us were reflections? Were there infinite possibilities for variations on the me theme? My head ached. Maybe this was just a mental aberration from a stroke (neatly explaining my now-throbbing migraine), and I could save myself the infinite calculations necessary to come to a viable theory.

It was mind-boggling, and when this Sarah pulled away and saw me misty-eyed, she took it for joy at the prospect of immanent parenthood. I didn't have the heart to tell her otherwise.

"I wasn't expecting you this afternoon—you pulled such a long watch yesterday, I thought you would be wrapped up in your experiments all day." Sarah's innocent comment pointed me in a less emotional direction.

"I couldn't wait to see you any longer." Her eyes gleamed at my words. "And Richards is so proud of your capacity to produce viable eggs, he all but chased me toward you."

Sarah laughed (this time I knew it for sure—though the uninitiated would still think she was hissing). I felt a fresh pang at the ease with which she mimicked the Sarah of my world.

I was still squeamish about the leathery surfaces of the eggs on the rocky floor—especially when I saw a small shiver in one of the eggs off to the side of the cavern. Sarah tracked my eyes and gave a little trill of satisfaction.

"I'll need to move that one in a few minutes," she murmured, and glanced up at me in that sweet, coy way I was accustomed to.

I understood she was asking for my help, but she confirmed it, saying, "Even in the six hours since you last shifted the eggs, their weight has increased substantially. I was worried about being able to shift them on my own."

I had to access this form's memories again to understand more of the biology of the saurian race. It was confusing to be me, and not in any way human. I didn't even know how much I should work to acclimate to this new world, and life experience, since my ultimate goal was to return to my original space-time. But I decided it wasn't fair to those in this space-timeline not to have my care and support while I was here.

So I moved closer to the egg in question. Up close, I could see striations in the leathery skin, and assumed that was part of the growth pattern for this child. Sarah stood beside me and massaged the surface; stroking the growing being inside, not dissimilarly to the way human women rubbed their engorged wombs. I joined her. She smiled again, and I felt that dangerous palpitation my own Sarah knew how to induce in me. It was a moment of wishful déjà vu, and yet, here I was bonding with an almost-mate over her offspring— that were purportedly also mine.

It was too much to process, and I was feeling less and less a man of science, and more and more the awkward, socially immature geek of my early teenage years.

In those days, my mom had suggested I join her at her Bible study group to try to place myself within a greater context. She was a woman of great faith, but every time I found a new contradiction between passages, the more removed I felt from her circle of understanding. It wasn't long before I concluded that document was nothing more than the delusional maunderings of possibly well-meaning, but mostly misguided men. It didn't help that there were contradictions in various translations: that cemented my opinion that there was too much humanity in what was presented to be a reflection of the divine.

College general education requirements forced me to take a religious studies survey course. It opened up several more interesting vistas, which I pursued via a handful of philosophy courses. Those appealed to me most because of their effort at logical reduction. But though the question of whether there was an almighty, unknowable Being as root cause to human experience had stopped being a joke to me, I still wasn't comfortable enough with any particular religious framework to commit to a regular practice. I certainly wasn't the weak-minded sort to submit to the blandishments of some priest, or pastor, or mystic. So I kept my feet firmly planted on the scientific path.

And it had led me to exciting discoveries that did tend to confirm some mystical unknowable. I appreciated the Buddhist perspective on withholding judgment until the evidence of my senses could confirm my beliefs. So I soldiered on… and now was trapped in this strange predicament that indicated there was far more to investigate than anyone I knew had ever suspected there might be.

In the meantime, my philosophical musings seemed particularly apt, as Sarah and I worked together to negotiate the egg onto its other side. The thing was bulky and massed at least 40 kilos, so I could see where it could take multiple individuals to manage the correct care to ensure a healthy… hatching? Emergence? I still didn't know enough about this biology.

Sarah nattered on about the various visitors she had welcomed during the day—individuals I had known, or at least vaguely recognized, in my own timeline. I had to marvel again at how perfectly aligned these two realities were, regardless of how divergent the species' physical forms might have been. How could humans and reptiles be both so alike and so dissimilar? Who could have imagined that there was a way of perceiving a soul that would allow the same personality to express itself in such a different context?

In fact, maybe it was the perceptual question that would help me return to the space-timeline in which I felt most at home.

Sarah looked at me from behind yellow iris with cat-shaped pupils. "Mark? Why don't we cuddle up over there?"

She nodded toward the warm wall in the cul de sac of the tunnel. "Come, relax with me. We won't need to shift the eggs for a while now."

I wasn't expecting it to be comfortable, but I misjudged the lizard form I inhabited. It was akin to sunning on the beach in my old form, crouched down on the rocky surface, leaning against the rough wall, with Sarah curled against my side. The radiant heat was relaxing, whether it was infrared (as in this case), or reflected in the visible spectrum (as I was used to from home).

"I hope you don't mind if I close my eyes." She yawned.

"Sure! No problem. Hefting around those eggs would take it out of anyone." I was glad for the comfort of her unfamiliar form leaning against me, soon drifting in to the deeply relaxed breathing that bespoke restful sleep. I needed time to assess where I was, and how I was going to proceed. I didn't know anything about the nature of this transition. I needed an experiment that would jostle my realities again, so I could consider my options with more clarity.

Chapter 6

By the dimming light at the mouth of the tunnel, I determined that sufficient time had passed that we ought to shift the next egg. I nudged Sarah's shoulder enough to get her bleary-eyed attention. When she saw the angle of the light, she sprang up, fully awake, whatever analog of adrenaline our bodies possessed running through her veins in full force at the thought of mishandling her children.

"You ought to have woken me earlier." She chided me as we stood over the egg, looking for handholds by which to move it.

"You needed the rest." My eyes slid away from hers.

"You got caught up in a new experiment idea," she accused. She knew me too well—even here. She caught the movement of a shadow in the entryway and pressed her lips together. This conversation was not done, but would be shelved until we could be alone again.

It was her crafting partner, Karalynn. Sarah lit up at the sight of her friend. Karalynn bustled in, all business. "I didn't think you would have help tonight, so I came to check on you."

Karalynn glanced at me, uncertain. "I didn't mean to interrupt anything…" Her voice trailed off.

She was too perceptive for my comfort. "You're not. We were just tending to our duties."

"I brought you a nourishing casserole; I didn't think you would have had time to scrounge up any food, and you really do need to maintain your strength to carry these to term." Karalynn whipped out a knapsack that had been hidden behind her bulk, equipped with a tablecloth to protect the food from the dust on the cavern floor, and a luscious-smelling dish—that looked completely unappetizing to my human-conditioned eyes. Not only that, but I had to actively refrain from chortling at the inadvertent matches of human and lizard idiom. I was getting punchy from this experience of bizarre magnitude.

The women eyed me askance, and I worried anew that I was not actor enough to pull off this kind of deception. The form might help me blend in to this reality, but I had no cultural context for these interactions—at least not without an android-like moment to access this body's memories. It was that moment of removal that would always undermine my presence and authenticity in these experiences.

We sat down to Karalynn's impromptu picnic and I resolved to enjoy it, visually unpalatable as it was—certainly I had never enjoyed gelatinous ooze as a meal before. It was restorative, though, and for that I was grateful.

I was also grateful to fade into the background as the women chattered about their projects and friends. Under the guise of thinking deep, scientific thoughts, I was able to gain a new sense of the values of this society. Again, I was shocked at the number of parallels between our two civilizations.

I could feel the insidious pull toward this female, who shared so much in common with the woman I had just married in my human reality. I struggled with whether I should give in to those feelings, since my goal was to return with all possible haste to my original reality. On the other hand, the me in this reality had obviously seen the merit of attaching itself? himself? to this woman too.

Neither of us would want to wound this woman.

Having reasoned my way through this thorny emotional issue, I congratulated myself and returned to the flow of conversation. I noticed both of the women shooting me covert glances; what had I missed? I took my cue from Sarah's coy glance.

"Karalynn, thank you so much for bringing such a tasty meal and supporting us this way."

She took my subtle hint, and made happy noises as she repacked her picnic materials. As she bustled out, her tail described small, happy arcs through the air. I couldn't remember whether I had ever had to take that kind of lead in my home reality, but it seemed a bit of a departure from the norm.

I put it out of my mind as Sarah moved slowly toward me. Her eyes were soft and wide, and locked on mine, as she closed the distance between us. I was helpless to move; mesmerized by the way her golden irises were swallowed up in her ever-dilating pupils. I was looking forward to learning about this new physicality under her tutelage, but felt awkward as her arms reached up and her hands cupped my face.

I would never forget that kiss, though.

I decided that night that I could at least satisfy my scientific curiosity about this new location. My decision, though, held no sway over my altered reality; this was only the first of my hops through space-time.

Chapter 7

I didn't have much choice about where/when I was, and when I would be propelled forward into a new experience.

I was content in lizard space for just long enough to bond with Sarah, and get excited about the imminent arrival of our offspring. I was spending mornings in my lab, puttering with some new equations, nibbling at the edges of what I had been working on in my previous reality, and trying to avoid the fatal flaw that had forced that experiment into meltdown.

I still didn't have any information on what had propelled me forward, nor any answers on the mass collapse of our experiments, but I did have a theory that this reality might be protected from a similar experience because of the nature of our psi connections with each other. We had daily meetings matching the Scrum philosophy of project management in the human reality: five minutes where we were each given insight into progress and projects currently underway. It was surprising how often these meetings cross-fertilized our work and led us to new conclusions. I very much appreciated the time for input, reflection, and feedback with my team members, and understood at a fundamental level which paths not to pursue to avoid the quantum entanglements I now felt certain were at the root of the failure of my bonds to my previous reality.

Despite my care, and on a certain level, resignation to remaining in this new reality, shortly before our children were set to emerge it happened again. I was in the cave talking to Sarah, when my vision started going starry around the edges. Vertigo struck. I tried to remain upright, and Sarah rushed to my side to support me.

I didn't recognize the symptoms of the shift until I shook my head and realized my surroundings had changed again.

Chapter 8

I was in an open savanna. The grass was chest-high, and I couldn't imagine there would be a high-tech research facility anywhere in the immediate vicinity. The shrill screams of a prehistoric, winged beast shattered the eerie silence. I dropped to my knees, hoping to hide; my new incarnation was trembling with fear.

Another strange shriek sounded close to my ear; when I dared a peek, I noticed a harness on the beast's neck and muzzle. There was distant laughter as I opened my eyes further, craning my neck to see what was on the back of this thing that had landed so close to me.

A deep voice called out in semi-mocking tones: "I told you I had complete control—I can't believe you fall for the fake attack pattern every time!"

I looked up with a blank stare; he was human-like, but not someone I recognized. He was overly familiar with me, though, and I had to reach for jocularity to match his tone. "Not everyone has nerves of steel. Despite the harness, it could still throw you at any time. You're just an adrenaline junkie."

I searched my new brain for any information on this face, which was somehow familiar. To my shock, I discovered that, in this reality, I had a younger brother—who obviously used his birth position in the family to exercise every last death wish that might draw attention to him.

He leapt down from his perch and flicked the reins over the beast's back, slapping it on its flank in dismissal. He slung his arm around me and shepherded me to the tree line, sharing his excitement about the combination of drug therapy and behavioral training to tame the wild beasts that surrounded us.

"So you just have to use the right proportion of DMSO near their feeding grounds, and make sure you've got the saturation level right in the local herd, and they're docile enough to eat the meat right out of your hands." He glanced at me expectantly.

I decided to play along, though I had no idea what he was talking about. "So you had to test this yourself, and risk losing a limb?"

He snorted. "It's all in the name of science. I thought you, of all people, would appreciate that."

I had to grin. Though I'd never had a brother before, and worried that the existence of this one meant I was getting further from my reality rather than closer, I could appreciate this kind of sharing. I didn't even mind his left arm around my shoulder, and jabbed my arm with a stiff fist bump.

I had no idea where we were headed, but was grateful he seemed to have taken the lead. The sparse trees I had glimpsed from the middle of the savannah quickly developed into a true forest. The contrast between the heat of the sun beating down on my head and the cool gloaming of deep woods startled me into a surreptitious survey. A quick glance at my hands revealed a strange configuration of fingers—there was one missing on each hand. They were now arranged so I now had two sets of opposable digits.

I faltered, stumbling on the branches scattered on the forest floor. My brother reached out to steady me. He looked at me, perplexed. "You've never done that before. What's going on?"

Looking down at my feet, I saw I had no shoes—nor a fifth toe. I heaved a gusty sigh, and used the stumble as an excuse to sit down. "Must be the after-effect of the adrenaline rush you just inspired."

I tried for nonchalance but my brother wouldn't let it go. "I don't know what's wrong with you, but stay here, and I'll run ahead and have mom call the doctor."

I flapped my hands as if indifferent. "Seriously, it was hot out there, the sun and the mortal fear combined so I need a breather. I'm just feeling a little lightheaded."

Evidently that still wasn't quite right, since he took off at a run, moving deeper into the forest. Now I was well and truly sunk. I had no idea where I was or what to look for next, so could only await his return and hope that nothing in my demeanor gave me away any further.

I decided to take the opportunity to explore the rest of this new body to see if there were any other surprises. A quick investigation inside my pants revealed man parts that weren't entirely unexpected. I did notice there was minimal body hair. My smooth skin and fine body hair had me exploring my scalp to see whether I was bald. Just random stubble there.

Come to think of it, my brother was also bald. Maybe this was a species-wide circumstance? My arms and legs were a little more tan than what I had been in my previous human body—at least what I could remember of it after such a distance of experience. I worried about other things I might be forgetting, but had to tamp that down as I heard quickly approaching footfalls. The doctor's thick head of hair disabused me of my hairless assumption.

As it turned out, our home was built in a tree—though calling it a tree-house could call to mind unsophisticated child fortresses that in no way matched the complexity of this aerie. I could see the utility of the extra sets of opposable digits on both hands and feet, given the way we were expected to approach our home. And I could see that claiming vertigo would be a serious cause for concern, given the falling hazard from that high up.

So, I endured the poking and prodding and light-in-eyes flashing that ensued. I still downplayed the experience, and eventually the doctor had to concede that he couldn't find anything wrong with me. He did recommend that I stay home for a day or two, under the watchful eye of my family, to make sure there wasn't a repeat episode.

I sighed as he finally left, and my mother speared me with a gimlet eye. "You've been spending too much time at the lab, that's what the problem is. You have a wedding coming up, and you're still obsessed with your experiment. You're losing weight. You need to eat more."

She huffed off, and I sighed again. Maybe I would get another chance at a wedding night—though Sarah the lizard certainly hadn't left me in doubt of her affections while we were together in that reality. I had high hopes that I would soon meet Sarah in this reality. An enticing thought.

In my originating reality, it had been a few years since I had lived at home, so this fussing about was rather novel. I didn't know what to expect in the way of a meal, either, given that I had been acclimating to nasty variations on slime and slithery in my lizard version; it all tasted great, but wasn't so appealing to any other, human-conditioned sensibilities. Here, being in a body closer to what I was used to, I had to imagine that I might reacquaint myself with crunchy food, or even the firm flesh of chicken.

My mouth watered at the thought, and, as if on cue, my mother returned with a lap table and plate full of a range of delicious-smelling food. Looking at it, I saw a preponderance of green, and hoped that didn't indicate we were vegetarians. Nonetheless, I was hungry, it was satisfying, and I gulped it down.

My mother appeared satisfied with that, but still hovered, determined to worry about her son. Eventually, I decided to see if I could place myself more firmly in context. "When is Sarah coming over, then?"

I tried not to convey any urgency with the question, and had guessed wildly that if I were getting married, it would still be to the one woman who matched me at a soul depth.

My mom didn't blink. I breathed again.

"I suspect she'll be over after dinner again." Mom sighed. "I still can't get over that you're old enough to get married. That you will be leaving home."

She seemed melancholy. I could only imagine her discomfort—if I matched my human age, and had been living at home all this time… it would be an adjustment.

I tried comforting her: "It's not like you'll never see me again."

She snorted. "I know you need to move out, move on, move up in your career. It's just me being maudlin."

She got up to leave, but I held out my hand to catch her arm. "You know I'll always love you, right?"

I hadn't gotten a chance to see my mom at all in my lizard incarnation, and the loss was a thorn in my side. I was glad to be able to tell this version of my mom how much I appreciated her.

She smiled gently. "You're a good son. I know you'll be fine."

The sun was westering, so I suspected my afternoon plate had been closer to dinner than I had thought. I hoped that meant Sarah would be showing up any time now. I couldn't wait to see her again. It felt like it had been months since we had last been together, though that may be partly due to my longing for her familiar human form. I hoped I wouldn't be facing any shocks in that department, given my mom's apparently standard-issue female body. I wasn't sure how people in this reality expressed shock, and didn't want to offend Sarah with any inadvertent miscues. I leaned back into the corner of the comfortable couch and mused on what she might look like.

Chapter 9

Dinner was a formal affair, complete with different courses. It was in a dining room up a flight of stairs, and, I suspected, built on another tree. This time there was something that tasted like chicken, complete with crunchy outer surface typical of the battered and fried stuff back home. This was the sort of food I had been longing for each time I had endured another plate of slop as a lizard. I almost moaned in pleasure at the familiar texture in my mouth. My mom didn't miss my expression of bliss, and laughed.

"It's a good thing I've been teaching Sarah all your favorite meals, otherwise I'm sure you'd have convinced her to move in with us."

I wasn't sure whether to laugh or be offended at what sounded like a character flaw to me. Back home, I had become pretty well self-sufficient when I had gone to college, and I couldn't believe how coddled I was in this reality. It made me appreciate my brother's daredevil ways a little more.

He grinned at me from across the table, and my father chimed in. "Logan would've had a comeback for that. Cat got your tongue?"

Mom shot back, "He's too busy thinking about his wedding night, comparing it to the joy of a well-prepared meal."

I could feel the heat creeping up my neck. My family at home had never been this forward. I didn't know how to deal with this ribbing. I spluttered, and finally said, "I trust you all to respect Sarah a little more when she's here in person."

Everyone roared with mirth. I guess I was touchier on the subject than they expected. We settled down and finished eating without any further slurs against myself, or my intended.

While the knock on the front door was expected, I couldn't help the palpitations I got. My mom held me back, while my dad welcomed our visitor with full formality. I wondered at the pomp and circumstance, but then saw that this community was more conservative this way too—a strange dichotomy with the teasing that had taken place at the dinner table.

Sarah showed up with a full entourage: her parents and some other duenna-like lady whose ostensible purpose was to keep us from rushing into each other's arms. I'm not even sure all of what was said during that visit, as Sarah and I only had eyes for each other. Here, her eyes were a more familiar brown, and though her auburn hair was in some intricate up-do (and there seemed to be a lot more of it than she had worn in our original Earth experience), she seemed physically familiar to me. That brought its own satisfaction and longing, but I needed to focus on the business of the evening. There were documents to sign, and I was glad to take this as an indication that our marriage ceremony might be soon.

Studying the paperwork, I saw our wedding date was again 6/6/2012. I couldn't sort out how that might be the case; I had no idea what today's date was, though. I looked up, lost. Logan caught my eye and saw where I was on the form. He chuckled and announced to the crowd, "My brother is so lost in the clouds at seeing Sarah in the same room he's forgotten today's date. I don't know how he managed that, since it's the fifth! We're all planning to be at the cathedral at first light tomorrow morning to begin our vigil. He must be feverish."

He made as if to feel my forehead. I batted away his hand, and the rest laughed at his teasing. This time my blush was full-fledged. I would get my wedding again. I couldn't believe my luck. I wondered if my dislocation in time-space would only allow me to live within the narrow parameters of the few months around the original disaster—I noted that for further study. In the meantime, I was thrilled to see Sarah in something very close to her original form.

And I wasn't burdened with the thought that another consciousness had participated in the creation of our children. It would be all me this time. Still, I felt a subtle melancholy that I wouldn't see the product of what I had nurtured so carefully while in lizard form.

I was glad to see Sarah had a hard time concentrating on her paperwork too. I suppose, in a society where even adult children continue to live with their parents until they marry, a certain level of shyness is to be expected. I couldn't imagine anyone breaking free of the restrictions, either, given the way we were being chaperoned. How had we even managed to reach this point with this number of eyes trained on our every move?

I consoled myself with the thought that in 24 hours we would be man and wife; I vowed that this time I would not miss my wedding night.

All too soon, Sarah and her entourage left, the duenna in charge of the signed documents. Now I understood the formal meal with my family. We were preparing for a day of duty and ritual unlike anything I had known previously.

My mother shooed us all off to bed. I was surprised when this meant my brother and I scurried up several more winding flights of stairs to an outlook at the top of the tree. We still shared a room? And what about beds?

It took more acting skills than I feared I might have not to flounder in complete perplexity. My brother was still in a teasing mood, so didn't seem to notice. "You're still all starry-eyed from seeing her. At least give me a hand with the hammocks."

That explained the lack of beds, anyway. He continued, as I held one end of the rope contraption, "How did you know?"

He was opening a minefield for me, and didn't even know it. I finally resorted to saying, "I saw it in her eyes. The way she made me feel when she looked at me that first time; I'll never forget it, and I want that for myself for as long as I can have it."

It was the truth, as far as it went.

I was glad when he left his questions at that, since they made me homesick for "my" Sarah. Time was so much more elastic than I had realized. Now that I was bouncing between parallel existences, I had no objective way of knowing how long I had been separated from her, or my home reality. And it was looking like, if I could control my jumps, I might even be able to attend my original wedding night. That didn't alleviate the sudden, wrenching homesickness that rolled over me as we settled into our hammocks that night.

Looking out the porthole-like windows through the crown of the tree to the full moon outside, I may even have had to scrub my cheeks of suspicious wetness.

I consoled myself with the knowledge that Sarah was here too, and we were shortly to be married. I was glad Logan seemed to have dropped off into deep sleep and wasn't aware of my melancholy.

Chapter 10

As mom had predicted, predawn arrived much sooner than expected. I almost tumbled out of bed at the sudden squawk outside our room. Logan was only marginally better, mumbling curses to the prehistoric bird beating its wings to stay level enough with the window to peck at it—a living alarm clock.

We stuffed ourselves into clothes and went downstairs in search of food. Before I could feed my grumbling stomach, we were intercepted by our parents. "Remember: We're fasting until tonight when we celebrate with a wedding feast."

Logan and I groaned in unison. Logan tried to weasel his way out of our parents' oversight. He claimed care duties with his airborne steed, but our parents had made other arrangements with his veterinary team. He rolled his eyes at me and said, "See what I have to tolerate with you as the number one son?"

I buffeted his shoulder the way he had mine, yesterday, and he put the lie to both our ages by sticking his tongue out at me. My mother barked a stern "Children!" and we both looked straight ahead, blanking our faces.

Never having known what it was like to have a sibling before, let alone a brother, I was surprised at how easy it was to fall into the close bantering I had witnessed among classmates. Having seen the three offspring lizards that Sarah and I had created in that other reality, I decided we would absolutely have more than one child in this reality too. This sibling thing was too good not to share with the next generation.

My mom took another look at both of us, and shook her head. "Didn't you boys see the formal clothes I laid out for you?"

We both groused; I was glad it wasn't just me bearing the brunt of parental disapproval. She chased us off to the bathing room (and I really had to marvel at the engineering that allowed such a luxury somewhere halfway up a tree) with the exhortation not to come out until we were squeaky clean and ready to present an honorable face to those gathering for the celebration.

The butterflies started then. I had originally had a small wedding, with only our closest friends and colleagues. I didn't even know who might show up to this one, since I was now plus a brother.

Nonetheless, we were both quick with our ablutions, not wanting to be late. I discovered formal wear in this reality involved layers and layers of silk-like material. Something like a unitard underneath it all, followed by a fine undershirt and shorts, followed by an embroidered overshirt and pants, followed by a vest and kilt-like contraption, followed by a jacket. I felt duly trussed by the time my brother helped me into all these clothes. My main hope was that I wouldn't have to pee at an inconvenient time.

A consolation was that my brother was wearing the same stuff and (thankfully) had to pee first. Some surreptitious glances showed me it was just a matter of pulling fabric aside in strategic moves to be able to release the beast.

I supposed this was another expression of the conservatism of the culture: we should all have trouble reaching our privates, thereby being more likely to remain chaste. Which brought my thinking back around to Sarah. I wondered what she would be wearing. I faced a new round of trepidation as I imagined how I would achieve nakedness once we were alone tonight.

My consideration was interrupted by a sharp knock at the door. My father came in and sent my brother to be with our mother while he tended to the last details of my outfit. Logan lifted an eyebrow to me, and it didn't take psi talents to know he was telling me I would be sharing the details of this talk with him later.

I grimaced. The talk in my original incarnation had been awkward and stuttered through suffering jaws. And I now knew about sex in two different forms; I knew some of what to expect, and knew I was very much looking forward to bedding my bride. This father, though, surprised me. I suppose I should have known from the bawdy talk at the table last night that he wouldn't be shy about sharing details; but this was almost Too Much Information.

I was trying to avoid the implication that he had tried (and succeeded in) using these maneuvers on my mother. There were some variations on physiology here compared to human (and lizard) experience, and I never would have guessed how sensitive feet were, given the toughness of my soles—and the fact that they were exposed on a constant basis. I still blushed when my father spoke earnestly about the nature of being intimate with my bride.

Eventually his explanations came to an end. I was grateful to move on to the next portion of the day. I was curious about what a cathedral might look like in a tree-dwelling society that seemed to have the whole "harmony with nature" bit down much more so than my home world. In fact, both alternate "mes" lived in worlds that didn't have the pollution issues we had struggled with as humans. I wondered whether there was an alternate reality with humans, technology, and no pollution—if I ever landed there, I'd take notes on how to improve things at home.

Mom and Logan had already gone. Dad and I followed in the predawn, ambling slowly through the towering trees of the forest to avoid being drenched with the heavy dew. Interestingly, we descended to ground level to travel to the cathedral, and I wondered if there were a treetop conveyance or path, but couldn't ask without exposing myself. The first rays of sun created unexpected rainbows in the moisture, making the trip awe-inspiring.

I barely kept my jaw from dropping at the sight of the cathedral. I imagined Yggdrasil could be related to this immense tree: The bark was worn smooth by the caresses of generations of hands, yet the girth of the base was wide enough to hide a house. The carved edifice existed in the crown of the tree, some hundred meters in the air. There was a clearing around the whole, as if any other growth deferred to the tree's magnificence. Another hundred meters out was a ring of venerable old trees, standing sentry to the one in solitary glory. Looking closer, I could see a network of cables connecting the trees to each other and supporting the building in the middle.

I focused on the construction, and appreciated the overtones of baroque architectural features, with scrollwork and other embellishments adorning every surface. Where European architecture relied on stone, this was entirely constructed of wood. I didn't know whether that was because stone was scarce, or the weight would have been too big of an engineering obstacle to overcome. Once again I mourned my outsider status that I couldn't ask these things without raising more questions than I was comfortable dealing with.

My father led me into the clearing underneath this extraordinary construction. I stepped toward the largest spiral staircase I had ever seen. Dad grabbed my arm and held me back. He admonished me: "That's not how a man approaches his bride; he must be more subtle than that."

I looked at him in confusion. He grinned. Apparently this was a hidden part of the ceremony that fathers sprang on sons at the last possible moment. It was also part of the reason for the pre-dawn arrival—so nobody else could witness the challenge he was setting me.

Somehow I was meant to climb one of the trees at the edge of the clearing. Its boles were so large, ten men couldn't encompass them with their arms linked together at their hands. Having reached the unattainable height of 50 meters in the air, where the cables were attached in support of the flying structure in the middle of the clearing, I was then to navigate that web, find the hidden groom door, enter, and center myself in the groom's retreat for 8 hours of meditation and fasting.

I goggled at my father. How was I to accomplish this without ruining my finery? He laughed. "Take off all your outerwear and bundle it into this carrier."

It made a neat package on my back by the time he was done, but I still couldn't fathom climbing 50 meters up a tree with smooth bark.

He smiled again. "I'm here to be your coach, guide, and mentor. I did this to win your mother, so I'm positive you can accomplish the same."

Then he winked at me and brought me to a tree on the far side of the clearing. Since most people never came to the area by this direction, nor overlooked the obvious entry point, nor were even aware of this secret men's ritual, nobody noticed the discreet foot and hand-holds available on the tree on the far side of the clearing.

It was still going to be a challenge, but I understood the power of a ritual enforcing a sense of accomplishment and teamwork on this kind of day, so I smiled at him, too.

I made my way up to the dizzying height, and was thankful I wasn't actually dizzy. I didn't dare look down too much as I traversed the network of cables stretching between the trees. My father stood below, indicating the way forward. He couldn't save me, should I slip, so I stayed focused on my goal.

It almost came as a surprise to find myself in a small vestibule that reminded me of Japan—tatami mats, neutral-colored walls, and sliding doors with something like rice paper allowing in light, but opaque enough to keep my vigil private.

Someone had left a presence lantern, so I could see enough to attempt a cross-legged seat on the floor. I suspected that this body had received training in meditation. I, unfortunately, had not. I was full of nerves about today, with its many unknowns and rituals. I was sure they had been explained to me prior to my presence in this world, but that didn't comfort me now.

Dementional

I was glad, when, half an hour in, my father silently entered. I had been worried about trying to dress in my finery again, on my own, but he had told me not to worry, just wait until he showed up (by more conventional means) to help me prepare.

He placed a finger to his lips to indicate we were to honor the quiet time by not speaking further, held a basin for me to freshen up, and helped me into my formal gear. Then left as noiselessly as he had arrived.

I wasn't looking forward to sitting still for a whole day, ostensibly to meditate on the big step I was about to undertake. I had already married this woman once before—and lived with her post-marriage. I felt none of the trepidation most first-time grooms would.

Instead, I set myself the task of seeing whether I could access memories from this mind, and whether I could run a mind experiment on what would keep me from displacing realities again—unless I intended it, and was certain I could return to my original reality.

The first task proved surprisingly easy—and engaging. I'd never been interested in more than just the relationship with Sarah, and now wondered whether that wasn't a self-limiting function of having been an only child of older parents. We were introverts, interested primarily in the things we could validate through experience and experimentation.

In this reality, the community, again, was a much stronger entity than I had lived in my originating plane. I could see pluses and minuses to the strong interdependencies; I was glad even here I was studying advanced math, and its application in understanding our world and our universe. Despite the forest living, this community was also technically advanced, and I would be able to resume my research once Sarah and I were past the planned, month-long honeymoon.

My body's memories revealed themselves as being cellularly based, imprinted on the body that had experienced them. It made me wonder whether some of what I had considered psi talents as a lizard were an additional set of cellular memories. It was fascinating. I was sunk in a meditation, in which accessing the root physicality of my body allowed me to re-experience things like old wounds, and the first time Sarah and I had held hands here.

The real question: What was tying those new cells to my consciousness—or even allowing the transmission of the information to it? Was this evidence of my soul? Or was this psychosis?

As a side note, I could see the parallels between three different dimensions in how a new union was celebrated. Taking that as my starting point, I was soon dozing in my comfort zone, imagining taking my new wife into my arms once again.

That was how my father found me, late that afternoon: a little rumpled, with drool smeared down half my face. He laughed himself silly straightening me up.

I could hear movement out in the main space, and wavered on the edge of another bout of nerves.

"Son, you'll do fine. It's only people you know, or Sarah's family. We're all here to wish you well."

I had to grin at those words. Even if I were a little tongue-tied, it was all expected as part of this life-transforming ceremony.

Chapter 11

As I stood at the altar—a live tree stump with little twigs bearing barely unfurled buds—awaiting Sarah's arrival, I looked out across a sea of faces. I had never been in front of this many people in any of my lives, so was weak-kneed as Sarah moved toward me, the core of a beautiful flower of her closest family and friends, still mostly hidden by the swaths of cloth that connected them one to the other.

I had never seen such beautiful symbolism as she was literally expelled from the group to be reborn into a new family. The ceremony was blessedly short, and I didn't have to do more than respond to the officiant in the logical places before we were, once again, handfasted one to the other, a sprig harvested from the altar sanctifying our union.

The rest of the evening passed in the sort of happy haze where the majority of the memories are like an ultra-vivid snapshot of a simple moment: When my mom kissed Sarah and welcomed her into our family; when Sarah's granddad handed me a leaf he had saved from the tree under which he and Sarah's grand-mom had hand-fasted; the hilarity when my brother raised a toast and misnamed me as himself; even the special dance carried out by the children in the town as a reminder to remain joyful together.

I could see the focus on the symbolism and the importance of paying attention to details—though the culture that added them was vastly different from what I was used to. I had to wonder if that was part of why we still had prehistoric predators in this world. My brother had arranged a pterodactyl fly-by from his biology division colleagues, in honor of our ceremony; his confirmation of their classification underlined both my horror and awe at their immensity.

As the hours passed, I felt increasing urgency to whisk my girl away. I understood there was a bit of a conspiracy to delay our physical bonding, and I still wasn't entirely sure what the plan was to get us to our destination, when Logan showed up with Karalynn. "I'm ready for you any time, just let me know."

Looking across the room, we located Sarah—literally trapped behind a wall of relatives.

This was where the younger generation could counter-conspire: Logan and Karalynn took off, dancing across the newly opened dance square. They undertook a wild and high-flying set of steps that innocently caromed them off the older set hemming in Sarah. Amid the hilarity, nobody noticed as I rescued her from her family; we took off at a sprint down a side hallway, and out the back door.

I don't suppose it would have surprised me had we been caught out back, since I literally couldn't keep my hands off Sarah. It had been far too long since I'd been alone with her, and in a form that I understood. I had to caress her face, stroke her hair, nibble her ears, neck, and lips. I was all ready to compromise her on the back steps of the hall when she giggled.

"We have all night, and I don't want an audience for our first time together."

"What do you mean?"

She pointed: when I looked up… there was my brother, whistling at the moon from the back of his dratted pterodactyl. When I understood he was to be our ride to our honeymoon hidey-hole, though, I all but ripped Sarah's arm out of its socket hoisting her up behind me.

I was glad for the experiences of the morning to acclimate me to such heights without a safety net, because although Logan had rigged straps for both of us to be fastened securely to his beast, I suspected I would have screamed like a little girl at having done this 24 hours previously.

I was thankful the airborne service was brief, in any case. Logan's beast landed neatly in front of a cottage at the far edge of the forest. The quaint log cottage overlooked a cliff with a neat crescent of sand accessible below. We stood and watched as the waves crashed beyond the small bay, and out further, I could see the shadows of other islands.

This didn't look like anywhere I knew from my Earth experience. The abundance of islands looked like stepping stones from our vantage point. Certainly, from what I had seen of the maps at home, the evening before, it appeared that the crust had broken up more significantly in this reality. The entire planetary face was marked by small islands, hence the smaller communities and increased reliance on aerial transportation.

My brother left us. I was grateful that he was sensitive to my need to be alone with Sarah. I wasn't going to miss this edition of my wedding night!

Chapter 12

This Sarah was different than her other-world selves, more innocent. I was going to enjoy reacquainting myself with the girl I had fallen in love with worlds, and years, ago. My bride was wide-eyed at the full moon over the bay, and we decided to bring a cocoon of bedding out onto the promontory. We breathed in the fresh air and let the pounding of the waves below soothe us into a relaxed and loving state.

We also had to sort out how to remove the elaborate layers our families had swathed around us.

By the end of it we were giggling. The clothes' fastenings were set in ticklish zones. When one of us would reach around the other, the second would squeal as we discovered more and more spots sensitized to each other's touch. I suppose the clothes were designed that way; an innocent introduction to exploring each other—though I hadn't laughed this way while my brother and father had helped me into them.

We forgot the blankets we had set up outside once we were na-ked. We had started down a path that would lead to an irrevocable joining, but first we enjoyed the simple touch of hand on face. We moved closer together, and I could feel the heat radiating from Sarah's body. Sarah had always been naturally sensuous; even here, in her innocence, it held true. She was unselfconscious in her skin. I breathed in the scent of her hair, and sent it cascading down her back, having finally located the last of the pins holding it in its elaborate coiffure. We were at ease in each other's presence.

Not to say she wasn't coy, glancing at me from under her eyelashes, as I skimmed my hands down to her waist. I brought her that last inch closer to me so she could feel my arousal.

A bed without blankets invites closeness and exploration, and we took our time. My father's words were still ringing in the back of my head, regarding the importance of focusing first on Sarah's needs—the more ready she was for me, the more easily we would bond. So I went slowly. I was glad I had experience with this from other worlds, otherwise I could well imagine a fresh-faced young man could get lost in the sounds and scents his beloved would start to produce.

When she was panting and straining against me, she finally took the initiative, grabbing me by the waist and pulling me close. De-spite my experience, I was not prepared for this. All of a sudden we WERE one. We were in each other's skin; we were in each other's minds; we were united on a cellular level that excluded any other awareness.

Finally I understood that there was more to sex and lovemaking in this world than in others. We truly were bonded. We were still bound together in a timeless ecstasy as the sun crested the ridge.

It was almost a religious experience, feeling our way not only into each other but also into the world around us. It was only the sun warming my back that brought me into a broader awareness again. I was concerned I had done her harm, but as I moved, and the sun warmed her cheeks, her eyes fluttered open, and she blushed becomingly at me.

With the return of awareness and movement, we discovered that sometime in our bliss, the blankets had been returned to us, our bed draped in floral tribute, and our kitchen stocked with a nourishing breakfast.

On one level, this mortified me: Someone, or worse, a group of someones, had spied on us in our intimacy. On another, it did recall the old bedding ceremonies in medieval Earth, and verified our fully fledged status within the community. Now, we too would be eligible to advance our careers and take votes.

I sighed while Sarah was washing up in the bathroom; there were so many things to get used to when visiting these alternate "mes". And I was still no closer to solving what had blown apart my connection with my birth plane—though, after last night, I didn't want to leave this existence. I couldn't fathom what our biology here had elicited. I had never felt more connected to anyone, or the world around me, than I had the previous night.

It was a mystery that was to remain unsolved for the moment, as Sarah came out fresh-scrubbed and modestly dressed. She handed me a pair of shears without a word, and turned her back to me. I was perplexed until she brought her hands up to hold a hank of hair for me. She wanted to proclaim her choice by changing from a child's length of hair to an adult's. It tickled me that she would ask me to do this.

I couldn't resist asking: "Are you sure you want me to do this? I have no experience cutting hair… and your hair really is beautiful."

She laughed: "Are you chickening out on me? Backing out of our agreement? This much hair is such a pain to take care of—especially when I'd much rather spend the time with you."

I bussed her quickly on the cheek and snipped where she had indicated. It was still much longer than what she'd had on my original Earth, but the result was a cute bob that brought all the latent curls to life. Sarah laughed, and tossed her head to set her hair flying.

"Excellent! Let's eat. We can play with hair later; I'm starving now."

"Absolutely. I saw some crusty breakfast rolls in a basket in the kitchen; you look for the preserves and cheese."

We set on the food with voracious appetite and caught up on the insignificant details that had led up to the momentous event yesterday. As it turned out, once we had gone from dating to engaged, the rules of society had clamped down on us. We truly hadn't been alone together for months, and had had to rely on coded messages designed to pass through the multiple filters of family and friends to assure one another that we were on the right path together.

It was an exhilarating discovery to find she had been missing me as much as I had her. The day passed quickly again to night.

Chapter 13

I was, in a way, glad when people came to check on us; the whole bonding/merging thing at night, while amazing, had me so blissed out during the days that it was hard to imagine accomplishing anything mundane. Still, there were only two visits: one from my brother at the halfway point through our seclusion to replenish our supplies; and one from our parents, at the close of the month, to welcome us back into the community.

Sarah and I looked at each other, confused, as our parents led us to a new part of our village. "Where are we going?"

My dad smiled at my question. "Be patient. We have a surprise."

I shrugged and reached out to hug Sarah close. Wherever we were headed, my home was with her. I wasn't watching my parents anymore, I was basking in the aura of Sarah's happiness, and caught the tantalizing flush that flooded her face as her feet stopped walking. "What's wrong?"

"Nothing. Look!"

I looked around, confused. Finally, my eyes settled on our parents standing in front of a large tree with silly grins on their faces. "What's going on?"

My dad ceremoniously handed me something that looked like a door handle. "To accept our gift, you need this."

"Gift?"

Sarah elbowed me. "Don't be stupid; look up!"

There, above us, was a freshly built construction. Now that I was paying attention to something other than Sarah, I could smell the fresh scent of wood shavings and sealant. And our names were carved into the base of the tree, in the formalized curlicues I recognized as echoing those at the cathedral.

"Wow. Thanks!" I had to work my throat to choke out the words.

My dad thumped me on the back and handed me the handle. "Here, put this in the front door to complete the construction."

Sarah and I climbed the winding stairs up to our front porch. I made her squeal as I swung her into my arms and carried her over the threshold. That's where our parents found us, kissing once more.

"Here now, there's plenty of time for that later. Pay attention. You need to know where things are."

Sarah's dad was gruff, but proud to point out which features had been contributed by whom. "See, your neighbors knew they wanted another fancy front nearby, so they built the main reception hall and porch—complete with woodworking embellishments. We knew Sarah was trained to be a good cook, so her mother and I worked on putting together the kitchen."

My dad chimed in next. "I know you're most interested in the bedroom, so that's our contribution."

We all laughed at that. Sarah spoke for both of us, then. "This is the most amazing surprise I could have imagined. It must have taken more than a month to build, though. When did you find the time?"

Her mom snorted. "It wasn't that hard; we've all learned how to work well as teams after half a lifetime together. You'll find it comes easier for you too. It will be up to you to expand or redecorate as you see fit."

That first house together took on great meaning for both of us, and truly cemented our relationship to our town. We wouldn't be looking further afield to settle down. We understood the ways our community had come together to welcome us into the fold as a new householder unit.

We had another day or two at home to acclimate ourselves to our friends and neighbors, while finding places for all the gifts that kept appearing mysteriously on our doorstep. There was so much joy in finding a hand-crafted set of dishes, or a hand-loomed set of sheets, that it felt like our wedding ceremony wasn't yet done. I was reluctant to leave my cozy haven to attend my first day of work. I didn't want to leave our cocoon, despite the fact that I knew I needed to earn our place in this society.

So we avoided consummation for the first time since our marriage, and held each other through the night. It was fitting that there was an oppressive atmosphere, and impending storms, when I left in the morning to return to lab duties. I supposed I shouldn't have been such a grouch, given the generous vacation I had been granted (at least according to my Earth's standards), but none of my colleagues were Sarah, the most important element of my life—the person I could count on, who wouldn't change despite the many changes I was enduring.

So I tolerated the fun at my expense, and plowed through the accumulated messages and memos that had come in during my absence. Here too, I was surprised at the turn technology had taken. Our networks were organically based, taking advantage of osmosis and photosynthesis to translate information simultaneously across the globe. We were literally in sync with the moods of the planet. Having experienced the bonding, I could see where this had some logic to it as well, and had to marvel at the innovation that would lead to using plants for communication.

I hoped it meant that I could find and repair whatever quantum-level tear had sent me careening through two shifts in reality; an organic intelligence should be able to reconnect me with my original vibration. It was an interesting theory, but I put off exploring it because I was so fascinated with this version of my wife.

When I got home that night, she rewarded me with a new glow. "Mark? I have news."

"Hang on, I haven't gotten to kiss you yet."

She laughed, but cuddled into me to welcome me home. "I went to see Margene today."

"Yeah? Who's she?"

"Silly! You know, the town's midwife. I'm pregnant."

"Seriously? Wow—that's great!" I was thrilled—maybe this time I would be here long enough to meet my offspring. I worried, though, when she counted out the months for me: gestation in these bodies was close to a full year. It was a biologically expensive undertaking that formed yet another underpinning for the societal decision to keep its children at home under close supervision for at least three decades.

It also meant that the whole community was now focused on the task of taking care of Sarah. She had only been my wife for a month, but the low birth rate and long gestation meant that everyone was invested in taking care of her. I no longer had much more than the short nights in which to hold her, and take care of her in ways strangely reminiscent of our lizard selves. Everyone needed this to end well; not many women here were able to bear live young after such an arduous gestation. It also explained my brother's high standing in the community, despite his bachelor status, given his investment in the biological sciences.

My wife's expanding girth, and the families' and neighbors' involvement, meant I spent more time with Logan again. I was grateful for his insights into our biology, as well as the connections we shared with nature.

The conversations underlined my suspicion that there had been something fundamentally out of sync on my Earth that allowed us to break apart the sub-atomic particles that should have prevented my kind of displacement. I was on the point of sharing my predicament with him at least half a dozen times in our conversations during those months, but each time, stepped back from that precipice. I worried I would alienate the person giving me such valuable insights into the natural world.

Instead of sharing my concerns, I threw myself into research. I learned about the quantum connections between living things through their morphic fields, and fretted about the details of biological impact on my elegant math equations proving the Higgs boson. I was sure there would be a way to use the membranes on the outer layers of plants to conduct a safer experiment that might allow me to reintegrate with my original body.

The months flew by. I was excited that I had managed to stay in place for so long, and congratulated myself on having calmed the quantum excitement that had tipped me into this wild ride. I was going to witness the birth of our child this time. I was going to be able to return to my original Earth and original Sarah to integrate all these lessons to the betterment of all our realities—at least, that was my grandiose thought.

I was secretly writing my Nobel Prize acceptance speech. I was an ass.

Sarah's confinement arrived in due course, though I could hardly believe we had already been married a year. Time had a way of slipping through my fingers that left me dubious about my original intention. I was happier here than I had ever been on my home Earth. And yet, Sarah's accouchement was a scary prospect. I knew, all too well, the dire statistics governing live births in this reality. More than likely we would be facing heartbreak. It was time for me to find faith and pray; integrate some of that morphic-field theory with the reality of what we were living.

Giving birth in this version of Earth was in many ways a cross between what I had seen in the lizard world and what I knew of live births on my home Earth. Sarah had gestated her egg inside her body; the birth process would be not unlike a hen laying a fertilized egg. The challenge would be to keep the egg at the same temperature as Sarah's body for just long enough that the shell would become brittle and we could rescue the child from within. Too short, and tearing the shell off would damage the child; too long, and the child would suffocate. It was, as I said, biologically expensive.

I was a nervous wreck.

We had installed special space heaters and an incubator equipped with sensors to let us monitor our child's health. I remembered old Earth stories about water birth, and incorporated that innovation to our incubator: Water is a better conductor of heat than air, being my main argument. We were still working out the details of how the egg would become brittle while surrounded by fluid. I thought we could get around that by keeping the incubator only half-filled with water, and rotating the egg every five minutes. Even the midwife was impressed with the level of detail I had invested in working out this new contraption. I just hoped it would be enough to tip the odds in our favor.

Margene said the birth was going well. She had enough experience with these things that I trusted her assessment. It didn't make the waiting any easier, though. If my brother hadn't taken me outside for a walk, I suspect my pacing would have worn a groove into the living room floor.

Expelling the egg was all Sarah's effort. There was nothing I could do to hurry it along. I didn't want to stray too far from home, so we walked in circles on the forest floor until I couldn't hold myself back anymore. I rushed back up the side of the tree to burst through the door. I heard Sarah groaning in the bedroom. There was no need for me yet.

I went back to pacing, and Logan gave up on trying to distract me. Even the admonishment that it would be my job to take care of the hardening egg couldn't settle me down, or convince me to conserve my energy. Listening to Sarah's labor was almost too much to bear. I couldn't imagine how it would be possible for her to remain unharmed by the size of egg she was expected to produce.

Finally, I exhausted myself enough that I settled onto the couch, and dozed off. A sudden flurry at the door startled me awake, and I saw Margene smiling in the doorway. Her beckoning wave propelled me forward as if on wings, and I rushed into the room to see Sarah's dazed but smiling face.

And then I saw the egg. It was almost luminescent, with a pearlized sheen to its outer layer. It looked otherworldly in the water bath with the heating element trained on its surface. I slowed my pace and hesitated between kissing my wife and inspecting the egg to see whether it needed turning yet. "You're amazing."

Sarah smiled. "I know. Give me a kiss then go check on our egg."

How could I not obey? Sarah's cheek was still damp with sweat; even her lips tasted salty. But curiosity drove me quickly from her side.

I reached a tentative hand toward the shell, and thought I felt the world shifting around me. I was frantic not to miss this moment, and rushed the last inch to touch the surface. Looking back on it, I should've paid more attention to the other symptoms of the shift, because it was sheer adrenaline that caused me to be unsteady on my feet. Luckily the midwife had expected this kind of reaction and batted my hand away, while my brother caught me by my shoulders and supported me in regaining equilibrium.

I almost snapped at Margene when she led me through a few breathing exercises before allowing me to approach again. Slowly and gently, I reached out to rest a fingertip against the surface of the egg. The surface was as smooth as glass. I couldn't sense any movement within. "Is it supposed to be this still? I don't even see any ripples."

"Don't worry about it. So far this is all within normal parameters." The midwife tried to reassure me.

"The birthing process was as exhausting for the child as it was for Sarah." Logan had his own perspective to add.

I looked over toward her, and saw her chin drooped against her chest, her breathing slow and regular.

I caressed the shell. It was hardening beneath my touch. I got so excited by this progress I began rubbing the entire exposed surface. The midwife cautioned me about rushing, but her own testing indicated we would probably do well to shift the egg on its axis. It was large enough, and heavy enough, that I marveled that Sarah had carried this within her womb for so many months; it required both my brother and I to heft it carefully to expose the other side.

The doctor stepped forward to read his monitors and test the shell's readiness. "Hmmmm."

"What do you mean, hmmmm? What's going on?"

"Your innovations seem effective. If you want, you can start tapping against the shell to see whether any striations appear. I like how quickly and evenly the shell is hardening." He was grinning as he handed me a silver-handled, pick-like tool.

"Start gently, to see how the shell responds."

My first tap was tentative. We heard it echo with a hollow sound.

"More firmly." The doctor urged me on: It was the perfect hardness to respond to my effort. My next tap was more authoritative. I saw faint lines appear across the surface.

"Try another area of the shell."

This time a crack broke through. Inside, I thought I could see the faint outline of a limb. Encouraged by this, I hammered away, all over the exposed surface. With an unexpected percussive sound, the shell shattered—and laid bare not one, but two infants.

The doctor and midwife bustled in close and picked up the babies. Margene said, "Ooh, look, this one's a girl."

"And I have a boy!" The doctor grinned at me.

The sound of the shell shattering had roused Sarah, and our eyes caught. With tears in our eyes, we held out our arms, waiting to receive our precious babes.

"Are they supposed to be this quiet? Is everything OK?"

The doctor approached with a swaddled bundle for my inspection. His smile assured me that all was well, and I discarded an Earth-bound, preconceived notion about noisy newborns. I could hardly fathom that this Earth produced infants so differently from what I had heard horror tales about during my original nuptials. I wasn't about to question my good fortune at this stage: I had helped birth these babies and I was still in this reality to enjoy them with their mother.

The doctor was inclined to stay and chat regarding the inspiration for the water bath to hold the egg, but I was anxious to be alone with my new family. I'm afraid I was a little rude shooing everyone out of our house, but the secret smiles playing at the corners of their mouths told me I hadn't crossed any irrevocable lines—and, in fact, was behaving consistently with other, proud, new parents.

I felt I had more reason for joy than anyone suspected: I was living through a strange, extended Groundhog Day experience in these parallel dimensions, and I never knew when to expect a reset. Having already been through two of these, I hoped I would soon regain control of the quantum entanglements and return to my original home. I expected each shift would last longer until I could return safely. I didn't even consider the anomaly that each experience had been better than the last, and had given me small clues about ways I might be able to fix things in my own reality.

So, that night we slept with the children in our arms. I was given another extended leave to help raise my children; I had never had so much time off before. The two little ones filled our days with wonder and alternating periods of activity and sleep. In the quiet hours of the night, I fretted that I wasn't monitoring my experiments or formulating new theories about how I might return to my originating dimension, but always managed to rationalize my inactivity as deference to the children's needs.

After all, in the history of our town, there had only been one other recorded instance of twins. Everything about this experience was unusual for our community. I wondered whether it was a reflection of my own bifurcated energies, but again maintained my silence on that theory.

Chapter 14

My brother and Karalynn were frequent visitors, and were immensely helpful in setting us up with a nursery and a regular sleep schedule. Their unity of purpose gave them an unusual closeness, and Sarah and I both speculated and hoped that this might develop into real feelings between the two. My brother's fascination with the twins related primarily to his background in biology. The uniqueness of his insights in that field occupied a good many of the conversations under our roof.

Given the normal inclusion of chaperons when young people were together, Sarah and I colluded to give these two more privacy than was normal, in the hopes of getting them to recognize the spark we hoped we saw. This was the idealized family life I had previously assumed would be out of my reach; I had always, before, been that Type A driven guy, reaching for the next promotion. In fact, I marveled at the dramatic change in my personality. I couldn't tell whether it was because of the children, the completely alien social structure, or because this society demanded that its members pay attention, first and foremost, to fertile couples and their children. Or even whether sideslipping through dimensions was stripping me of some of my defining characteristics.

Whatever the case, I noticed how much more I was able to share with Sarah. She was coming perilously close to understanding that my soul wasn't quite the one of the man she had initially been interested in—but she also regularly professed her feelings for me, so I wasn't worried about competition from myself, either. Still, I was young enough and inexperienced enough—even at whatever level of 30-something I had ended up as—that I hesitated to say anything direct about how I felt.

In this string of extraordinary days, feeling dissociated from myself through the unaccustomed activities of my life, Karalynn and Logan announced their engagement. My happiness was complete. After the celebrations that evening, with the children tucked in to sleep, it felt like the right moment for a tender proclamation. And yet, all evening, I had felt off-balance. I had almost asked if someone had cooked the food with an unusual ingredient, but since nobody else seemed to be suffering ill effects, swallowed it down as an excess of emotion.

We snuggled together in bed, and I marveled again at my luck with this woman. I could lose myself in her eyes, whatever form they took, and she always seemed sympathetic to whatever I wanted to discuss. I cradled her on my chest, stroking her arms and back. Then I noticed a strange sensation spreading through me; the sparks at the edge of my vision announcing an impending shift.

I stuttered my declaration to Sarah, but found my arms were empty, I was lying in a gutter, and rain was splashing on my face. I was glad the weather masked my tears. Why had this happened to me? Why now? Why had I been so complacent about trying to find an answer, knowing I was in a dark-matter-induced state of entropy?

Chapter 15

If my circumstances weren't miserable enough, I felt hung over in the aftermath of this shift. Sniffing myself as I struggled to stand, I decided this body was suffering the aftereffects of a bender. I saw vomitous matter nearby and splattered on my raggedy clothing.

"Wonderful. I'm a drunk. And I have to try to find Sarah. Again." I rasped sullenly to my feet.

A horse-drawn carriage pulled to a stop in front of me. Sunk in my own misery, I paid no attention to the booted feet that stopped on either side of me. Then I was hanging in the air, hoping that the swirling in my head portended a quick shift to better circumstances. I looked blearily from left to right, and saw two uniformed men holding me up by my upper arms. Here, we seemed fully human, with the normal number of fingers and features, but for the life of me, I couldn't guess who these individuals might be. Or why we were in an age with horse-drawn buggies.

Blinking to try to clear my vision, I thought I saw streetlights. And power lines. What in the world was going on with the horses? And why were my thoughts circling so erratically? It felt like my brain was on an old-fashioned turntable and someone kept switching the speed between the 33, 45, and 78. I noticed the carriage was black and labeled with official-looking insignia.

I was then dumped in an ignominious heap on its floor, with the door slammed on my feet. The implication hit me with the force of a thunderclap: I had just been arrested.

I had never been jailed. This was humiliating beyond measure. I couldn't fathom the possibility that I would ever have existed in a plane where my unusual intelligence hadn't been fostered. My other two slips through the energetic discontinuity had landed me in happy fantasies; this was more like a nightmare. I still didn't have full control of my mental faculties, had no real options for improving my clarity other than to wait out the hang-over—and no real measure of how long the hang-over might last, since I hadn't ever felt this poorly. I wondered if there might be other changes in my physiology beyond the obvious surface similarities with my old human body. Certainly, looking at my hands, the skin was roughened, darker, with blackish-brown patches that could have come from some sort of dirty manual labor, none of which put me into the scientific hierarchy I was used to inhabiting. It might be much more difficult to conceal my other-worldly origins in this reality. If I had been an uneducated laborer, just opening my mouth to express my opinions could generate a whole new level of awkwardness.

I decided that for the time being I would keep my mouth shut, and live out the mulish mood that was settling on my shoulders. I could at least schlep myself to the wall of the carriage to avoid the worst of the jouncing over uneven roads. I didn't try to straighten my hair or scrub my face, to avoid creating any impression different from what was apparently expected from the condition in which I had found myself. Nonetheless, ten minutes of an uncomfortable ride was enough to make me increasingly nervous. I had no idea what to anticipate—or even how much longer I might need to endure the ride. Now that my bladder had made itself aware to me, I worried I might have a new reason to stink before being transferred wherever we were headed.

My worries eventually lulled me to sleep. When the carriage jerked to a halt, I awoke. How long had I been unconscious? I still felt uncomfortable in my own skin, and now suspected I had lice to complete my litany of woe. I tried not to scratch a hole in the side seam of my shirt as the back doors of the carriage were flung wide. I was blinded by a spotlight pointed directly at my face, and was so disoriented I couldn't place the grunts and mutters from outside the carriage as human speech.

Just when I thought I might be asked to advance under my own steam, two more uniformed individuals joined me on the bed of the carriage, easily lifting me from where I had curled against the wall.

Were these "people" as human as they looked? They were hefting me around as if I were a featherweight—which I might have been in my original Earth body, but this one had an enormous beer belly.

Cold air hit me as we exited the vehicle, and any bladder control I might otherwise have had escaped me. My captors guffawed in braying tones to see this evidence of my shame and debasement. I hoped there was nobody here who actually knew me, but in the next moment a face thrust itself in mine, and I cringed to recognize Richards—glorified as the epitome of a petty tyrant.

"So. You couldn't keep your promise, and now you can't even hold your water. You're a filthy mess. I've been assigned to make sure you haven't spilled any state secrets with your drink." He sneered at me while delivering his assessment.

I suspect we would get inverse enjoyment from whatever came next, when he ordered Frick and Frack to tote me into the facility. The emblem on the outside of the building matched what was stenciled on the conveyance. It also bore striking resemblance to the shields each of these individuals displayed with evident pride on their chests. Trying to keep my hands from betraying the tremor of fear Richards' words inspired in me, I shoved them into my tattered overcoat pockets—and discovered a similar shield there.

My confusion must have been evident, because Richard laughed again: "Poor little pretty boy forgot his curfew again, huh? This time Sarah won't be able to cover for you: She was here the whole time and we can prove your need for a drink kept you occupied for at least 48 hours."

My heart sunk to my toes. Sarah and I were an item here too, and I was in this state? What was wrong with me? Apparently I belonged with this cadre of goons, but they weren't like any previous colleagues I'd had. And why were we talking state secrets in the open when I was obviously in no state to counter any accusations.

By the malicious gleam in Richards' eyes, he had waited a long time for whatever comeuppance was due me now.

I didn't have much choice but to go where Frick and Frack dragged me. I did try to periodically lift one foot and then the other in a vague parody of walking. We proceeded down a tangle of halls, and the turnings and passages soon slipped the grasp of my addled mind; there would be no way for me to find my way back outside should that become a necessity.

We arrived at an intimidating holding cell. A bare bulb hung from the ceiling and hovered low over a single wooden chair. The men strapped me onto that unforgiving surface. A modified seat belt and manacles at wrists and feet kept me in my place. I don't know whether they had some evidence of Houdini-like escape artist abilities that they were so thorough, but it didn't give me much hope that I would get out of whatever they had decided to do.

Trussed up, trousers clammy with my own urine and clinging to my legs, I couldn't imagine what further degradation might come my way, but given the creative turn of mind in every previous Richards' mind, I despaired.

And waited.

Floodlights had greeted me outside and now I sat in a windowless room. I had no idea what time it might be. I couldn't even gauge time by the activity level in the halls, since the science facilities in which I had previously worked had always been sparsely populated. Each researcher kept his or her own hours and was independent of a normal, working-day clock. So while I had seen a handful of hastily averted faces, it could have been anywhere between noon and midnight on either side of the day.

My stomach started grumbling after what felt like the first hour of incarceration. By then, I was losing circulation in my hands and feet.

The chill in the room made me shiver, as the sensation of my clammy, dirty clothes competed with the itchy feeling of bugs crawling on my skin. It would have been nicer to assume the carriage had been purposefully infested with bugs, than admit I was likely responsible for the disgusting state in which I found myself.

I tried to treat it as a meditation challenge, but after the second hour without a visitor, interruption, or any relief, I began rethinking my decision not to speak—after all, I must have had some education to warrant the badge in my pocket.

I tried to wriggle around enough to find a less-wet spot for my legs, but the bindings didn't allow enough room for much movement. I managed to shift the chair enough that the light was no longer glaring in my eyes—I had enough excuses for a headache without adding the harsh light to the list. I half hoped that the noise of the legs of the chair scraping against the floor would call attention to my situation. But more time passed and no one came to check on me.

My stomach growled. I saw the tremor I had earlier attributed to fear, shock, and anger, was getting stronger. I had the nasty suspicion that the reason I still had the headache and was now shaking, was because I was enough of a lush to need time to dry out. Lovely. I couldn't even trust my own body not to betray me, and who knew what kind of misperceptions would be introduced by the drugs floating through my system?

The more I considered my state, the more I felt lucky to have avoided broader exposure. I was embarrassed; this was no way to live.

Eventually I did hear the staccato rap of heels striding down the hall. The footfalls didn't sound as heavy as those of my original captors, and I started to get excited despite myself. They paused outside my door. The door eased open with a great deal more caution than it had been shut, and I had the sinking feeling that this visit would add to my mortification.

A coated female figure backed into the room. I wondered briefly whether there might be blood work or detox drugs in my future. My speculation died unborn when the woman faced me, and I looked into Sarah's eyes. Hers had unshed tears standing in the corners, and I was unmanned at her disappointment. I hung my head, even as she walked toward me. I couldn't face the condemnation I deserved; I didn't even understand how I could have ended up in this circumstance.

I was surprised when Sarah leaned in and kissed my cheek, brushing the hair back off my forehead. She seemed more sympathetic than disappointed, which threw my confusion into high gear.

"I know you were trying to forget those experiments," she murmured.

She must have sensed my confusion.

"I see you've done a bang-up job wiping your mind. Just never forget I'm here for you." She ducked her head so I could see her face. And her tentative smile.

If I hadn't stunk to high heaven, had a face rough with who-knew-how-many-days'-worth of stubble, and could almost feel the lice jumping on my skin, I might have ducked in for the kiss she seemed to be inviting. As it was, I felt filthy, and unable to share any of my secret joy at finding her here.

She reached inside her lab coat and brought out some kind of thick drink, holding it to my lips. It tasted pretty good, despite reminding me in color and texture of Pepto Bismol. I hadn't realized how parched my mouth and throat had become.

I still had no idea how to break the silence that stretched between us. Sarah sighed and leaned in to kiss my forehead again before slipping back out the door. What would have happened if I had just opened my mouth? I would never know, but at least it seemed she had more of a scientific bent in this dimension. Maybe she could help me out of my predicament?

This third shift had evaporated any enthusiasm for exploring new worlds and new experiences with the people I had known from back home. Now I was just plain homesick. Why couldn't I just bounce back to where I had started?

I noticed a significant restoration to my faculties after Sarah left, and had to bless her again for the aid she had provided. It seemed whatever was in that drink rebalanced my electrolytes. I was no longer thinking in circles, and the tremors had all but stopped. Not that that was necessarily a good thing: now I really noticed the lack of circulation. The pins and needles were excruciating.

Chapter 16

Once again I heard footfalls in the long hallway outside my cell. This time, it sounded like the troops returning. I should have at least asked Sarah what time it was. Or whether I could expect food or a clean-up from my captors. Or even whether I should admit she had been in to see me. I groaned at the possibility that I would expose Sarah to something worse than lice if I inadvertently betrayed an illicit visit.

The door banged open and I tried schooling my features to a careful blankness, knowing that as bad as I was at poker in college, it wouldn't help me if Richards knew me at all well.

He might as well have been a panther pouncing on his prey; the moment he saw my face he chortled.

"I knew I could count on Sarah to find out you were here and do at least some of my clean-up work for me."

I wasn't sure what he meant by that, since Sarah hadn't done anything other than feed me the drink. I guess the mental clarity was to Richards' benefit too, though, so he would consider that as more important than a clean change of clothes or a shave. I suspect he delighted in having me at such an extreme disadvantage. His hair was black and parted in a line that looked like he had used a ruler, slicked with an abundance of gel, and carefully framed his clean-shaven face. I had never seen him with manicured hands or a tailored suit in three other incarnations.

He must have been at an official function, schmoozing people who could be duped into parting with vast sums of money to support his latest pet theories. I remembered he had tended that way on my version of Earth. In our infrequent staff meetings, he had spent most of his time reporting on the various sources of funding he had managed to bind to our research. My colleagues and I had laughed about it behind his back—very quietly.

Here, his level of self-importance seemed to have grown beyond mere bloviating to actual tyranny. I had no idea how I was going to handle this ticklish situation. After all, if he were going to do any research on me, it could very well prove our dark matter research was bearing fruit. On the other hand, would he even believe me, given my apparent efforts at self-sabotage? More worryingly, what had Sarah meant by suggesting that I might be trying to forget an experiment; I never did that. Was my pacifism being tested here? Were my ideas being subverted for offensive weaponry? Was that why the Richards in my reality had insisted on such strict segregation of experiments?

My head was exploding with questions. This version of Richards looked like he could hear my thoughts—his eyes gleamed as he stared at my face. Something about the whole set-up struck me as sinister. What if Sarah had been subverted here? What if she had fed me something that, Alice-like, had changed how things interacted in this reality and made my thoughts visible to others?

I almost retched again at the thought that a version of Sarah could exist who might sabotage me.

Richards finally spoke: "I trust that the formula Sarah whipped up for you is settling in and doing its work. I would imagine you'll feel the full effects in another hour or so, but in the meantime, we need to strip you so that as the lice die off they don't get trapped in your clothes. We wouldn't want to lose the data they've been collecting on you."

He was ambiguous about Sarah's role; I still couldn't find my emotional balance. The thought that the lice had been bioengineered to track my movement and body excretions was overwhelming enough. Processing the rest of his statement didn't kick in until Frick and Frack uncuffed me and dragged me to my feet. I needed their support: the circulation rushing back to my fingers and toes was painful, and I would have fallen over without their help. There was something suspiciously mechanical about the two men, especially now that I was seeing them through more lucid eyes.

Richards pantsed me while they held me up. The three of them all but ripped off my coat and shirt between them. There was no sympathy for my involuntary goosebumps as the coolness of the room hit my now-bare skin. I couldn't imagine actually working with Richards, or his goons, after this treatment, let alone after they propped me in a corner and sluiced me down with tepid water. I expected a cold after this, though my constitution seemed hearty enough despite the evident neglect I had foisted on this body.

Having messed up that holding cell, the trio frog-marched me to an adjacent room. They strapped me onto a cot and draped a light blanket over me.

"Sweet dreams." Richards smirked as he closed the door behind him.

What a blow-hard. Why was he so determined to keep me unsteady? I had even more questions swirling through my brain after this half-hearted attempt to clean me up. I hoped I'd shift soon to avoid the full repercussions of whatever the previous me had gotten our body into.

Once again, my dissociative thinking had me wondering whether all these experiences might be the natural result of fever dreams or brain trauma. I had no way of collecting data on the different bodies I had inhabited. On the other hand, I had experienced every sensory input I was aware of—and some I didn't normally have—during the course of this anomaly, and I would have had to rely on my senses to gather data in the first place. I was well and truly trapped in a catch-22.

For my own sanity, I returned to the theory that the quantum entanglements broken apart by my experiment's release of the Higgs particle was the source of my dimensional slips. Nobody had ever proven or disproven the case for a soul to be moored within a physical vessel. What if I were proving that by my experiences? What if the persistent presence of dark matter were the glue that held a soul to a physical reality? And, what if the dark matter were the bridge that connected all the realities? What if my attempt to detach a Higgs boson had been the equivalent of pulling the plug on my connection to my original reality?

I almost yelled Eureka at that thought. And just as quickly fell into a more troubled line of thinking: What if I had to replace THAT Higgs particle to get back home?

I must've fallen asleep after that, because the next thing I knew, a soft, warm form was curling up next to me. Sarah shushed me when she heard me draw a breath. This was new behavior. I was used to Sarah being more timid. Since neither of us were wearing rings, and I wouldn't have been attracted to me in my current state, I couldn't figure out why she kept coming back to see me. And her hands were making bold advances on my body under the shabby blanket Richards and his team had tossed over me. Since I was tied to the bed, there was nothing I could do to either discourage, or encourage, her continued forays. I essayed a whisper to warn her off, that we would be discovered, and produced a raspy growl. She put one hand over my mouth to enforce her wish for my silence. Then she replaced that hand with her mouth.

This was the fourth version of Sarah I had known—and the fourth to have unexpectedly blown my mind with the impact of her sexuality on my body. Once again I mourned the wedding night I had missed with my original Sarah; how different would sex have been after our wedding ceremony? This Sarah obviously knew the me of this body quite well. She drew out my pleasure as long as possible, and then sucked me dry to avoid giving any further evidence to my jailers. I assumed. When I could see straight again, and the ringing stopped in my ears. I couldn't believe how fantastic that felt; that I had never been blown before; that Sarah would do such a thing. Obviously, I was still thinking in circles, despite my earlier clarity. And the tremors were back. Maybe this would be a blessedly short stop in my sideways slide through dimensions and I could get back on the trail of that Higgs particle.

I took a deep breath to settle myself and calm my nerves. And then I realized Sarah had disappeared as quietly as she had arrived. I had missed my chance for even a furtive conversation with her. Or a shared smile at the connection she had forged between us.

My suspicions woke up again: What if that was just another way of collecting body fluids for testing?

I couldn't believe I was doubting Sarah at the least provocation. Hadn't she just proved the depth of her feelings for me? After all, who really enjoys the salty, tangy taste of cum enough to keep it in their mouth—or swallow it? It would only be someone who cared deeply who would submit to that unpleasantness. Right?

I decided to shelve the debate. Nothing would be resolved without Sarah's input. Direct input. I just couldn't shake the sense that all this sneaking around served a darker master. And, I had no idea who would have enough influence with Sarah to convince her to take these steps. Always in the past, we had been such an insepara-ble unit that she would have taken that kind of direction from me, not from anyone else. Unless the degenerate me of this world had told her to do these things before I had side-slipped into position?

That could make a devious kind of sense. But would he have ex-pected me to show up? What kind of experiment was he running? Maybe he had found a way to jiggle loose his own Higgs boson and was trying to create an open vehicle to be able to escape his own tether.

I would have jolted straight up in bed, but for my bonds. What if the versions of me that had occupied my body were trading places with the me that had vacated my previous location? What if the pervert who had trained Sarah to suck him off so diligently was now training MY Sarah to do the same thing? It was intolerable to consider. And yet, it was all me.

That, surely, was the road to madness. I had to figure out some way of thinking of my original self as but one reflection of the selves that had now all been unmoored. I had to believe that somehow, since we all mirrored the same person, we were all aware of the dislocation in ourselves and were all working to solve the problem.

Though… if there were more miserable "mes" out there, I could also see some of us working to sabotage that plan, in an effort to avoid returning to the hells we had left behind. Assuming that some element of randomness were at play within the infinite possibilities available, I could even calculate that a third would be likely happy to remain status quo, a third would be working for a return to the previous course, and a third would be working against anything changing again. The question was, how was I to convince the status quo set that it was important to fix this problem—without alerting the antagonistic versions of ourselves.

At least the math was soothing enough that combined with Sarah's efforts, I drifted into a restful sleep.

Chapter 17

Iwas undisturbed the remainder of what I assumed was the night, and woke feeling remarkably rested. Unfortunately, I didn't seem to have shifted into a new dimension, and my vision remained sparkle-free. While I was stiff from having been restrained in one position, I had retained full sensation in my hands and feet.

I wondered how long I would be stuck this way. It certainly didn't seem like anyone was in any hurry to listen to me talk. It occurred to me that I hadn't heard myself speak once in the, what… 24 hours? since I'd been here. I wondered if there were a reason nobody seemed to want to listen. Could I even speak? I tested my throat. I could clear it; obviously the structure was sound enough to support breathing and drinking. So I tried humming. I got an aberrant, gravelly rasp. That was peculiar. But then, I had been on a drunken binge and hadn't spoken since. Maybe it was just a matter of warming up the vocal chords?

I tried the classic "la, la, la, la, la, la, la". It sounded like rocks being shaken against a mesh screen. "Me, me, me, me, me, me, me" sounded, if possible, worse. I yanked and jerked at my bonds. I had to feel whether there were scars. Why didn't I have a voice?

A few minutes of futile effort didn't bring anyone to my rescue; now I had scrapes and bruises on my wrists. When I settled down, I supposed it would be possible to be injured or have vocal chord damage and not have scars as a reminder. It certainly explained why nobody was asking me to tell them much. I was glad I had enjoyed music class in my original body; I couldn't imagine the torment of not being able to rock out to something like "Sweet Home Alabama" when I really needed to get the endorphins flowing.

It was another incentive for me to hurry up and sort out who belonged where. But it was an impetus I could do nothing to sate without getting myself out of lock-up. How could I attract attention that would get me back to work on this problem?

With my voice being a non-factor this time around, I decided to try the meditation thing again. It was always hard to stop thinking about a problem long enough to clear my mind, but I had to find a way to create calm and patience while waiting for my jailers to arrive at whatever their decision might be.

Chapter 18

"Inman." Richards' resonating rumble murdered my name and startled me awake. Meditation must've failed me again; apparently I'd fallen asleep. Frick and Frack were back too. My stomach was growling loud enough they were sneaking sly smirks to one another behind Richards' back. I hoped the noise would make my request for me. The last time it had been fed was the thick shake from Sarah, and that wasn't sufficient to keep me going.

Richards was satisfied I was alert, and nodded at his assistants to unshackle me. They carried a plain gray jumpsuit and finally seemed to trust that I was able to dress myself.

"Your test results came back negative, so command has said you can be given limited release again." Richards grunted his own dissatisfaction with the verdict, but I assumed that meant someone valued something about my science somewhere in this complex, so my next task would be to find my way to a lab—I hoped it would be my lab.

Richards and his minions steered me down additional sets of hall-ways. I was never this confused in Alaska, and there was no natural light in those halls either. I wonder if I was missing some critical el-ement of my faculties in this environment. Thinking in straight-line logic, still eluded me, even after a day of drying out. Had I been that much of a lush before this intervention?

It didn't escape me, either, that Frick and Frack had snapped some sort of low-jack device to my ankle. It was the first indication of re-liable high tech I'd seen since my arrival, and I had to wonder how sophisticated it was. Would it report my movements in real time? How might it be disabled? Would it shock me if I strayed beyond the bounds set by my captors? And who were they, other than the enforcers who were now pushing me down hallways I still couldn't distinguish from the others we had already traversed. I was satisfied that my ability to generate an endless stream of questions remained unfettered. With that, maybe I had a shot at solving this puzzle.

Eventually, we arrived in front of a door. It was no different from any other door we'd passed, but this time, Richards made a show of pulling off the badge they'd put on a chain around my neck, over my head, and laying it flat against the reader in the middle of the door. The door opened with a click, then a clang. This seemed more in line with the high security I was used to. It looked as if I'd have access to the tools and materials I would need to continue my search for the Higgs boson.

Frick and Frack shoved me past Richards, into the lab, staying well clear of the space. Richards, himself, seemed curiously constrained to his side of the door and thrust my badge back at me. When I fumbled the recovery, he snorted again and dismissed me from consideration. The trio backed away and the door sprang closed behind them, apparently of its own volition. I wondered about that for half a minute before I realized it didn't matter if this space was programmed to reject certain DNA codes. Sarah might or might not be able to visit me here, but at least it looked like the gleaming surfaces of the work benches, the dry erase boards with equation notations, and the cabinets of calipers, Bunsen burners, vials, phials, and electromagnetic coils would serve me well. I didn't need the distraction Sarah would bring anyway. Especially if she offered another blow-job like last night's. I couldn't afford to be distracted with so much work ahead of me.

Since it didn't appear that anyone would be giving me any further direction, I wandered along the edges of the lab, confronting the equations the previous me had worked up. His hand was a little sloppier than mine—though that may be attributed to whatever palsy his alcoholic tendencies had introduced. For all his slovenly self-care, his lab was meticulous. I could easily follow the logic documented on the boards, and had no trouble deciphering the order of his materials.

And he had a lab I was in awe of: It was the size of a medium-sized lecture hall, at least forty feet square. There were five over-sized lab benches neatly arrayed in rows down the center of the room; two opposing walls were covered with floor to ceiling white boards. The far wall from the entry was edge-to-edge closets or cabinets of some slick, semi-reflective black polymer.

Further exploration revealed a cubby of an office opposite the wall of cabinets, complete with comfy leather couch and coffee machine. I still couldn't find a computer I would recognize as such. I wondered how the real data crunching necessary to verify any theoretical equations would happen without that assist. That there were no evident piles of paper assured me that there was some sort of digital help; I frustrated myself with my inability to puzzle out that resource.

I heard a distant chime. Was it a doorbell? Who might intrude that politely on someone labeled pariah by the powers that be? I went back to the door Richards had pushed me through, expecting to find an interface to buzz someone in. But there was nothing showing there. The chime sounded again. Where was that coming from? I walked quickly toward the far wall, which had seemed to be a long row of cabinets for research materials, and heard the chime a third time, louder.

This was worse than a game of Marco Polo! I didn't even know what I was looking for, nor how to respond appropriately once I did find it. Certainly nothing would be voice-controlled for me, given my voice's limitation to a gravel on gravel effect. I resorted to brushing each door with my fingertips as I walked past.

Touch worked wonders. Touch-prompts lit up on screens as I swept my hand across them. The chime sounded yet again; this time I could feel the cabinets jostling in sympathetic response to the sound waves. Some cabinets had materials for me to use in my investigations, one was a sanitary cabinet, one was a closet well-stocked with additional jumpsuits, and the final one was the one that was chiming at me: a food dispensary. This was more like it. I wouldn't care if it were served in bland cubes like some futuristic sci-fi creation. I was starved, and would be grateful for anything.

When the touch-screen registered my presence, it sounded a double-ding and showed a menu. Expecting bland, the list of gourmet options threw me. Did I really want to wake up my much-abused system with a spicy shrimp étouffée? On the other hand, maybe I should go for the rich protein of a good steak to replenish my energy. I noted that the upper corner of the display screen bore the legend: June 12, 2012, 22:00. That startled me too. I was back to the date of my original wedding ceremony? It was that late at night? Were we working off-hours night shifts here? I had been subliminally expecting breakfast, since it hadn't been all that long since Richards had deposited me here after having woken me up. The time, at least, matched the dinner menu I had been perusing.

If this dimensional jolt had followed the pattern of previous ones, depositing me close to the when of my original displacement, what had happened to the intervening days? I tried counting back, but gave it up as futile. There had been too many intervals of unconsciousness to come up with a reliable estimate.

The steak, when it disgorged from the dispensary slot at waist height below the screen, was piping hot, medium rare, slathered with sautéed onions and came with a baked potato and Brussels sprouts. This was the first meal in which I had recognized all the ingredients from my original reality—and they were prepared to my preference. It brought on another round of homesickness.

I could see the method to the dispensary madness, though: I'd missed more than one meal in a fit of scientific zeal—having an automated system chime at you until you ordered food would certainly fix that. It could also explain the contrast between my originally scrawny self, and the fat slab of a man-belly I could see obscuring my feet.

The apparent single-minded pursuit of test results did nothing to foster fitness.

Carrying the plate to my office space, I settled down at my desk to eat, and discovered that this too had a touch-based interface in certain positions. I was able to set my plate down to one side and start looking through my research files. I had to admire a system that forced everything into digital format from the outset; it made my workspace so much neater.

It also reduced the need for filing reports, since anyone with proper clearance and access would be able to see my results without any need for a separate request. Neat, not intrusive, but still more Big Brother than was comfortable. How would I be able to pursue my line of inquiry without setting off red flags in the system? It would be something to take into consideration as I continued. Meantime, I found relevant results from some of my present body's past research that opened an interesting road of speculation.

My problem was always going to be confronting the issue of the consciousness causing collapse of the quantum waveform I was observing. Since I had managed to side-step realities into alternate variations of myself, didn't that mean that, at some point, I was a non-corporeal entity who would be able to resolve that dilemma? (And thus neatly put myself back into Nobel consideration for solving one of the original perplexities of the quantum mind-body problem…)

The next time I looked up, not only was my plate clean (though I had no memory of cutting up the food and getting it to my mouth) but the clock in the corner of my screen said it was 0900. I still hadn't heard a peep from anyone or anything. Spoke too soon: The ding at the food dispensary recalled me to my duty to my body. I stood and stretched. I wasn't stiff. The conformable chair and ergonomic desk had allowed me to work the whole night through.

I shuffled back to the magic wall of food and other closets, dialed up a cup of oatmeal, and went to see about a shower.

That stall was as amazing as anything I'd experienced. I wondered in passing about the whole horse-drawn carriage bit outside the walls, since this steam closet had handy little depilatory drones and other automated scrubbing hands. By the end of my 15 minutes, I felt cleaner than I had ever felt, with the bonus of steam- and massage-enhanced relaxation. This truly was the life: all the scientific inquiry I wanted, no personal interaction, and automation to take care of all my bodily needs.

There was one problem: I missed Sarah. I missed all the Sarahs I had known. I wondered how the little ones were developing. I had to smack myself for not even knowing their names to properly memorialize them. All this time I had been so worried about getting back home, I had detached myself from the magic of my other lives. For now, creating a new theory of dark matter interaction would have to ease my pain. My literal science closet answered the youthful siren's call of investigation.

I had a tiger by the tail and couldn't afford to look around too much, lest I be annihilated in some quantum act of extreme exposure.

My oatmeal disappeared with the same ease as my dinner. I had no recollection of spooning the porridge to my mouth, though the bowl was patently empty, with a few stray oats on the side of the dish. I shrugged, deposited the dish at the dispensary, and stretched out for a nap on the couch.

I woke well-rested and remarkably focused, when the chime indicating a mealtime sounded at the far end of the room. This cycle agreed with me; I could keep this up indefinitely. I shoved aside the quibble about not seeing Sarah, and dove back into work.

Chapter 19

The next few weeks were much of a muchness. I ate when chimed at, slept when I couldn't work any more, and spent all my time adding to the equations scribbled on the white boards, annotating research results, and poking at mini-accelerator bits to try another take at shaving off a Higgs particle.

It was easy to get used to interacting only with inanimate objects; I certainly didn't want to hear my own voice, and in one of those moments of self-examination that intruded periodically, had the passing thought that maybe my voice had disappeared because of non-use. There weren't any personnel messages, assessments due, or any other of the minutiae that had frustrated me in the old Alaskan complex. In time, I would become an automaton in this facility. In some ways I felt like I was the goose being gorged for the sake of the delicacy of its liver—I could kill myself with this kind of focus.

When that thought became loud enough, I would spend a few hours poking through other files living in the server cloud that hosted my research. We were physically more segregated here than anywhere I'd seen, but that didn't mean I couldn't read some of what my colleagues were up to—or even collaborate across the virtual connections we shared. For some reason, it seemed face-time was verboten. I wasn't sure how that advanced our collective scientific purpose, but it made it easy to live more and more in my own head.

If it hadn't been for the forced time off in the previous world, or even the egg-gestating sessions in the world before that, I would have been hard-pressed to feel human interaction had enriched me so much that I wasn't happy to forfeit it for this level of cerebral existence.

Even those moments in the gritty gutter, and the fear of my incarceration in the initial hours of my life here, had faded to an insipid, gray memory. I had forgotten my questions about the extreme contrast between how people lived outside these walls as compared to the absolute luxury I perceived in the cloistered cell I had lucked into.

Then a new sound intruded on my focus: There was a buzz and a click as the door opened again. When I looked down at my screen, at the date, I realized I had been here for six months. I felt like I'd drowned in my rabbit hole. Looking up again, I saw Sarah. She was like a ray of sunshine in the monotony of my days.

She waved her hand and held her finger to her closed lips. This time I knew my voice was the culprit. Who would want to hear sweet nothings from the depths of hell? I took a step in her direction. It felt like moving through molasses. I couldn't figure out why I wasn't running toward her when it had been so many months since I had last seen her. Looking down, I noticed my belly was bigger than ever. At least this time I knew I had recently been scrubbed.

Sarah kept silent. The way she moved gracefully toward me, it seemed she danced to my side. She looked well, though there were hollows under her eyes. When she was close enough, she flung herself at me. A long separation should have done that for me too, but this wasn't my Sarah, just a facsimile who highlighted the ache of losing my home world.

Nonetheless, I took whatever version of her I could get, and happily held on as she grasped my bulk. When I tentatively stroked her back, I felt her shoulders shaking. That wasn't a good sign. Was she crying? I tilted her chin up so I could look at her face. There were indeed tears in her eyes. I was a cad for not having sought her out, nor having tried to escape my more insidious fetters.

So I lowered my head slightly. Leaned in to kiss her, wondering whether she would accept my wordless apology. She shocked me once more with her passionate response. This Sarah was more forgiving than mine—but then, I had never neglected my Sarah this way.

I knew I was absolved when she quickly stripped us both of our clothing, caressing my shoulders and back, and nibbling paths across my massive chest. I swallowed misgivings that this wasn't my wife; clearly, this installation did not foster close relationships, and likely we were intentionally separated from one another to create that artificial focus and drive that had absorbed me for six months.

Was this my reward for that much hard work?

Sarah grabbed me by my ears and forcibly yanked my head around. Her eyes bored into mine. She whispered fiercely: "I KNOW you! Don't retreat into your experiment. We've been apart so long, and I've missed you so much. Focus on ME for just a minute."

I met her gaze, and had to admit to myself that I couldn't see the differences between her and the one I had known. This time, there was no hesitation when I leaned in to kiss her. Her lips were soft, and moved against mine with assurance and ease. Her fingers reached into my hair and dug into my scalp. I had forgotten how her touch aroused me.

Our kiss deepened. Sarah seemed to want to crawl inside me. Her caresses whipped trails of fire down my back, and she hopped up to wrap her legs around my waist. I wasn't ready and staggered back, stopped only by the edge of one of my workbenches. Lucky for me, this one was clear of all experimental detritus, and I swung Sarah around so she was seated against the edge of the table. This was new for me in so many ways, but Sarah seemed satisfied to melt even closer. She was wet, and I slid in with no resistance. It was a shock to my monk-conditioned self, and it was all I could do not to cum that instant. Sarah moaned, and I lost my tenuous control.

Sarah shuddered as we climaxed. Now content, she huddled close in my arms. I couldn't believe she had gotten much enjoyment from such a brief encounter, but maybe she preferred intensity to endurance.

Eventually, Sarah caught her breath again, leaned in for a lazy kiss, and tugged me behind her to the hygiene cabinet. I wasn't sure we would both fit, but she was determined, and it was surprisingly comfortable even for two of us. She giggled at the settings I had programmed, and made some adjustments; even that seemed more domestic and effective than I had expected of her, here.

In fact, given the two times I had seen her here, I wondered how we had managed to get to the point of such sexual combustion. I tried hard to keep my thoughts from my face, but Sarah was as perceptive here as she had been in any world I'd known her. She leaned in and planted quick, butterfly kisses all over my face. "You've been the one for me since you helped me with my school work in fifth grade."

That was new: I hadn't met my Sarah until we were both in college. It was strange how some things were so similar here, yet our story's inception was different. Somehow we had grown up together, and had had formative experiences together that had impacted us on the deepest levels. I would have to work harder to respect everything this Sarah was to this version of me, despite official efforts to enforce our isolation.

I wondered if she knew what was going on with my voice, that it sounded like the barking of hell-hounds when I tried to speak. I still didn't know how to ask that kind of question without exposing myself for an impostor. I had to respect that this Sarah was passionately in love with this me; it would wound her too much to hear I was just a visitor.

Still, I could see the question in her eyes. Why hadn't I made an effort to find her? It was an open, valid question. During the previous two shifts Sarah had been my first priority. Was I that afraid of falling in love with all the variations of Sarah that I would retreat this far into my scientific isolation to avoid her for months on end? Shameful behavior for someone who had tied my life to hers in so many times and places. I would make it up to her. I leaned in and kissed her again, softly. I pulled back to form the words. My vision went starry, the prickles started in my hands and feet, and I knew I would lose this chance if I waited any longer. "I love…"

Chapter 20

I was falling through a vortex. I couldn't tell which end was up; the transition had never lasted this long before. Was this my opportunity to be the discorporeal observer? What should I be looking for? How did I even know I didn't have a body and we were just trapped in a whirlwind, slated for an early death? I tried reaching out to anchor myself, to anything, but there were extreme temperature fluctuations buffeting me. I couldn't sort out how I could feel those distinctions when I couldn't tell if I had hands.

Was this an entirely particulate world? How on earth would I stand being in this context for long enough to survive shifting the next time? There had to be little fingers pulling at whatever stuff of me was in place here; I felt like I was being torn apart on an atomic level. And where was my consciousness if my body were not a form I could recognize?

There were too many questions in the maelstrom of this version of the world. The pain was radiating from my extremities to my core.

It was overwhelming, and it took all my concentration to recognize myself. I must have blacked out then.

The next I knew, I was lying down. I thought, anyway. It felt like I was horizontal. I tried blinking. I was getting input from a spectrum of colors I had no names for. This looked like one of those psychedelic music videos with fluorescents and pastels competing for attention by swirling around each other. Settling into the new form, I flexed my neck muscles, thinking that would loosen me up. Instead, I flipped myself around. I was amphibian? In the water? Are you kidding me? How on earth would a being without opposable thumbs help me solve the most advanced theoretical physics equations ever created?

I couldn't even grumble. Here, again, I lacked vocal capacity. I would never again (if I had the chance) take the ability to express words for granted. I could blow bubbles like a champion, though. So I did. Someone had to be out there to understand I was mad. In all senses of the expression!

The bubbles muddied the waters and calmed down the crazy sensory input, and I could see there might be something tasty, dead ahead. This was weird. This body was more instinctual than I was used to. It darted forward, snapped its jaws, and swallowed. At least I didn't have to taste whatever raw, live being my mouth had just encased. If I thought about it too much, I would likely throw it back up, regardless of what this beast thought. Sushi. It was sushi. I could live with that.

I decided to see if there were a way of shutting down my senses and relaxing into this body the way I had with the lizard body. It was challenging, since I was so literally out of my element. I wanted to sit, or breathe, or lie down. The best I could do here was a cross between floating and wallowing; I still couldn't sort out the mechanism that was aerating the body's blood. Did I have gills? Was I poking a nose above the water? This was more confusion than I wanted.

It was distracting, too, to sense currents of pheromones floating by, and know there were others of this being's kind in the near vicinity—and closing fast. I wouldn't have any chance at survival if they were territorial. Maybe I would get lucky, and the disorientation washing over me would mean a quick shift out of this disaster in the making.

Of course not. I managed to flip myself end for end, and face the onrushing peers. Here again, I could tell: those two were my parents, and those two were Sarah and Karalynn. How to handle this? If they thought I was still me, they should be arriving just to say hi, right?

I was starting to understand some of the wavelengths as communication bands. This was a lot like the lizard body; we were all more attuned to a group mind that could share information rather than an individual perspective. Apparently, my bubble-blowing had broadcast on a broad spectrum, and my friends and family were rushing to rescue me. Embarrassing.

This Sarah more than made up for it, though, by brushing up against my side and settling, full-length, against me. The body heat of her leaning against me warmed me in so many unexpected ways; it was hard to concentrate on the communication process that soon swirled around me. I was grateful it had been so easy to find Sarah again, though, at the same time, still distressed that I had to sort out a whole new biology. It would have been helpful to have a Logan around, too, since we all seemed to carry over similar interests across lives, and he could have been counted on to give an in-depth analysis of how we were designed, and the way we used the physical traits we shared.

If we were amphibious, that could even mean there were eggs nearby. I had so many questions gyrating through my head; I could hardly settle myself. I certainly couldn't follow whatever communication was surrounding me. I earned the thwack Sarah's tail delivered to my rear end.

Reorienting myself, I found that bodies surrounded me on all sides. My mother was anxiously poking me with her snout, passing an electric sensation over my skin each time she pushed against me. Were we related to Moray eels? There were so many oddities and discontinuities; I didn't even know how to respond to that parental prompt. So I scrunched further into my skin, and put my snout on the short forelegs I discovered below me.

It must have been some sort of appropriate signal, since the level of turbulence subsided, and I started to understand the various modes of communication. The shared heat was to make sure I hadn't overchilled my body; apparently that was a source of a certain kind of confusion or madness in our kind. The snout nudging was electrical, in the way that defibrillator paddles were intended to regulate human systems. And this group of close friends and family had flooded the area with pheromones to help ensure privacy and calm.

They loved me. It was overwhelming to know they would go to all that trouble on my behalf, and I knew I had to make an effort to show them their efforts were bearing fruit. So I assayed a sentence: "I'm fine; thanks for your help."

I'm not sure it came out exactly right; I got some strange looks. But at least everyone backed off and seemed ready to let me sort myself out.

My forelegs weren't much more than vestigial appendages—a little more than fins and a lot less than hands—so I couldn't reach out the way I normally would have, to keep Sarah close. Processing the fact that I had a tail, and Sarah had used hers effectively to get my attention, took another minute; I made a tentative twitch with it in her direction, and she seemed to understand the intent of the invitation. With her close to me again, I felt more the master of myself. I wasn't sure what I was going to get out of this experience of life—aside from a new appreciation for opposable thumbs. I certainly didn't see any possibility for real scientific research at this level of development.

After the intensity of the work I had invested in my previous dimension, though, it was perversely pleasing to face the prospect of a bit of a break—with Sarah, again.

I didn't take into account that this new body had its own electrical generator field and an intrinsic ability to perceive a sub-atomic level. With Sarah settled next to me, I discovered we were sharing thoughts in a psi pool similar to what had been available in our lizard selves. We were learning things about the play of matter and particle that were deeply fascinating. I could well imagine why biologists on our earth were perplexed by the frequent torpor of amphibious beasts. From my new perspective, this stillness became highly active as we sorted the multitude of sensory inputs.

It also put a whole new spin on the sentient being question. If I were me (and I suppose that really was still open for debate) but I was in what scientists on my version of Earth would call a lesser-evolved form, did that mean I was less evolved here? I still had Sarah as a mate (though no way to verify whether that had been cemented with any sort of ceremony), some sort of circle of friends (after all, Karalynn had shown up too when I had appeared to be in distress), as well as an ongoing relationship with my parents.

In this body, I was able to perceive a broader array of spectra, and had an in-born ability to generate and interact with EM fields that I had always groped toward in my human form. My initial dismissal of the experience I might garner here might turn out to be unwarranted cultural superiority; certainly I was gaining more insights into how various elements of the electro-magnetic spectrum interacted with one another. Their activity seemed to broadly mirror the Brownian motion on the atomic level, as well as the significantly more difficult to pattern, sub-atomic level.

The dance between particles and waves was mesmerizing, and reminded me of an old weaving demonstration Sarah had dragged me to in Alaska. The way the shuttle had disappeared temporarily between the weft and the warp had been mildly interesting at the time—but even though I had put a good face on being pressured to participate in a trip to investigate one of Sarah's interests I was surprised that the old image had popped into my mind as a comparison. I must've been paying more attention than I had thought, because suddenly the whole metaphor grabbed my attention and wouldn't let go. What if the particle I had jogged loose were like dropping a stitch? What if I had unraveled a whole tapestry with my action? Even the seemingly disparate versions of myself could just be different-colored threads that happened to lie close to one another in creating a greater image of myself.

I was surprised at how poetic I was waxing. I was generally more focused on dry, scientific fact, and not so much putting it into a pictorial context. I suppose it could even be argued that this being, who was at home both in the water and on land, was balancing research and art in equal measure, bringing different talents inherent within me to the fore.

It was sobering to consider an amphibian superior to my human self. My lizard self had had the psi capacity for telepathy, which was one additional sense. This form's ability to manipulate matter on such a micro level through EM field vibrations made me feel like a superhero. And Sarah played with me, tossing me new wave forms, making our learning fun and an integral part of our relationship.

I remembered the Saturday morning cartoons with the old-fashioned white, pulsing circle images indicating mental, or other, force-at-a-distance impact, and amused myself for a whole morning by sending out regular, geometric-shaped pulses of my own. I could form whatever pulse I wanted: circular, square, star-shaped, rhomboid. Those artists had been so limited in their perception of how energy could conform to a pattern, my silly game felt like a new world of discovery.

Even my relationship with Sarah had taken on new meaning. We were electro-magnetically matched, and had complementary pheromone sets. Our biology predestined us one for the other. Where I had missed Logan earlier, I discovered the swampland that made up our home had interconnecting pools, and it was possible to reach him energetically, several pools away. Our parents were central to us, as well as all the 50 or so other siblings who had made it to adulthood.

Given my only-child status at home, this news alone was mind-boggling; how did all these extra sets of consciousness tie in with my previous experience? Would I even be here long enough to meet all these individuals? How would I know how to interact with them appropriately? Surely amphibians didn't have the kinds of family ties that humans did—although, hadn't my parents only just answered that question?

Despite my connection with Sarah, an anchor that seemed to carry across wildly different dimensional experiences, I felt lost. Each shift forced me to re-evaluate previously unconscious perceptions and took me further from my original home.

At home, we had joked about putting on the professional mask when we arrived at our labs, but here I was, literally, putting on the mask of new bodies every few months (at least as far as I could tell), and it was dissociating me further from myself. I could talk about my bodies as being separate from me. I knew what it felt like to have to integrate cellular memories with conflicting mental/spiritual carry-over from other dimensions. I didn't have a belief framework that allowed for a spirit outside of or apart from a physical vessel, yet these jumps kept underlining how deluded I had been in that perspective.

I remembered deriding a colleague for his so-called conversion experience, and his claim that there was something greater than, or outside, himself. Now I wished I had questioned him more closely. What if I couldn't find root in any dimension again? Was I destined to repeat these few months in an infinite variation of worlds and dimensions? If so, it sounded pretty close to a purgatory I had never claimed to understand—or even accept. And I still had no guidance for how to approach the problem, or support system, as I meandered my way through the multiverse like a pinball flung by a random application of force.

Chapter 21

As usual, Sarah was the one to sense my discomfort. It was easy to lean into her care, and subsume my inner loss of footing with the intense need to be with her. And a codependent willingness to give her needs priority in an effort to make more sense out of my life.

In fact, this amphibious set of selves—hers and mine—as biologically entangled as we were, provided the first real perspective on her experience of my erratic being. It's not an experience that has a useful vocabulary, and in more than one dimension I'd been in, psychoanalysts would have been more than happy to label me schizophrenic for detaching mind from body so distinctly; hence my caution about discussing it. Here, there were so few boundaries between us, and our language was not constrained to words, as such—defined, limited, and able to box you into a corner you hadn't intended. So, Sarah's questions, while uncomfortable and difficult to answer, were at least clearly articulated—insofar as you could describe a cloud of pheromones and EM fluctuations as being articulate. It felt much more like answering an algebra equation, where I was solving for X and filling in the blanks of her experience of me.

In its own way, it was not dissimilar to the sense of union I had had with her two or three jumps ago (I still didn't know whether to count the longer-than-normal shift into this dimension as a separate jump). The previous jumps had been in the pursuit of fertility and propagation, but this felt more like the pursuit of a necessary puzzle-piece of myself. As if our yin and yang expressions were only complete in the presence of the other. As if all our thoughts and experiences only made sense when there was a secondary lens through which to view them and bring them into focus.

When Sarah understood my half of the perspective, rather than rejecting me as an impostor, she rejoiced in the knowledge that we were but one iteration of a successful pairing across multiple worlds. I was flummoxed at this response to what should have been mind-boggling news, but then, I had just spent days fascinated by the interplay between the micro and macro currents in EM waves... because those features were built into the body I was in. Considering Sarah had lived a whole lifetime in this kind of body, maybe I was the bumpkin for seeing myself as a potential threat to the stability of worlds.

So, we worked together to modulate frequencies. I loved her more than ever, and I didn't have to worry about the words, because my feelings were part of the connection that bounced between us. It clouded the water around us and told anyone who entered our part of the swamp that we were a mated, committed pair. We didn't need or miss company, because we had each other, and the area around us was a new kind of laboratory—both for exploring the waves and particles floating around us, and for exploring the depths of our feelings, and the way those impacted our environment.

It felt like we were clicking on so many levels; I almost forgot my underlying quest. So it was truly a shock when, once again, feeling in my extremities started to dissipate and stars clouded my vision. I couldn't cry out in this form, but I knew Sarah was feeling my distress as I fought the current of change—as I felt hers. The last connected thought I received was: "Who will he be after this?"

Chapter 22

The blurring between one form and the next was always a shock to the system, and generally involved some length of unconsciousness as my spirit conformed to its new vessel. It was akin to being given a new set of gloves: sometimes they were fitted for children, and fitting in required a metaphoric shrinkage. Other times, as in the next jump, it was akin to being given a snow suit when you were used to just the gloves. I had no idea what to make of my new sense of self—it felt planetary.

Here I was, contemplating the size of spirit, and I knew there was no science to assess the mass of a soul. There was no science to prove its very existence.

Mentally breathing deeply to settle into this vast expanse of self, I tried to wrap my consciousness around the idea that I was experiencing whole ecosystems as circulation. I was being given a whole new comprehension of how subatomic particles traveled and interacted, since they flowed around my bulk the way scents flavor the air in smaller bodies.

My real concern was: how would I perceive relationships in this form? I still needed to find Sarah. How do planets have relationships? As it turned out, there really was no need to push that question further, as I felt the impact on this self from another being: I had a moon, and she was Sarah. An interesting variation on the symbiosis we had shared as amphibians. Her pull on me was undeniable, and had an obvious impact on the things that happened on my surface.

Here again, there were no words to limit communication. It was liberating, and felt like the information Sarah and I had shared and worked through in our amphibian selves had translated on a sub-atomic level to an immediate understanding in our planetary selves. We could make micro-adjustments in the speed of our rotation, and relative distance, and enforce cataclysmic change on the beings on my surface.

It made me laugh to see this new perspective on some of the old Gaia-worshiping cults of my Earth. They may have had a valuable insight, but would they have been offended to know they lived on a male planet? For that was the one constant in all my jumps: I was always my male self. I was always paired with my female counterpart, Sarah. Given the scientific fact of homosexual inclination, how was it that I was so consistently hetero? Was it a self-limiting characteristic of some of the narrow-minded constraints under which I had operated as a human? After all, who could say that a planet was male? There was no procreation between a planet and its satellite. And there were planetary bodies with multitudinous satellites—did that make those poly-amorous beings? If so, did that speak to my earlier question about my own self-limitations?

I had thought it would be difficult to communicate in this vastness, but discovered a different pool of connection than the water that had provided my surroundings as an amphibian. Space, itself, was as crowded as a subway station at rush hour. Planets, stars, satellites, comets, asteroids; we were all each other's brothers, sisters, parents, and lovers—each in relationship to another, but connected in ways apart from what an exoplanetary scientist might accept as logical. It came down to another expression of EM fields and the ether in which we operated. It helped that geological time operated at a pace that logically should have blipped me into, and out of, that body in a matter of moments, were my experiences solely mapped to a human perception of time. It seemed instead that each being's ability to measure its own movement and pace governed the length of my experience in that space-time.

I was beginning to feel less like a being randomly buffeted among experiences, and more like I was on a cosmic quest for understanding the interconnectedness of being. Where my human self would have rejected expansion beyond certain parameters, I had learned from my lizard self, amphibious self, and now planetary self, that perspective was what you made of it. I had gained valuable insights just by being in those forms. Previously, I would have felt that was impossible without extensive experimentation following the "work to disprove it" path of the scientific method.

I reveled in my world building. I could rearrange mountains like I was moving furniture. I could support new life as if I were growing hairs on my body. And I could start over with a quick tidal wave or eruption. I felt invincible. I couldn't understand how a planet could allow itself to be anything but, given the proper family of support surrounding him.

Of course, in that arrogance I was pursuing my own karma: I had forgotten that a large enough asteroid is appropriately called a planet-killer. So, when a being I somehow still perceived as Richards came caroming into my system, I was prepared to take on an assign-ment, or report on my learning. I was not prepared for a full frontal assault: or the experience of my own mortality.

And yet, body-less, I was not annihilated. I witnessed the mourning of my friends and family, the way their orbits destabilized and col-lapsed—a careful choreographing to avoid mutual destruction, and at the same time a drawing-in to protect what remained. I could see the asteroid belt I'd become; Sarah's remnants subsumed within the mass of debris, both of us enshrined together in the reliquary of rocks.

I didn't even know if, because there were still physical elements of my former body there, I was still tied to that space-time (or, really, have any sense of what space-time that might be). I couldn't con-trol any of the movements in that floating, dispersed field of rocks, nor did I have any sense of connection to it, other than in the most conceptual, abstract way. I knew intellectually that I had been that stuff, but couldn't be upset at the loss of the vehicle either.

It occurred to me to wonder if this was my real chance at being the incorporeal observer, and to find and replace that missing Higgs boson. Would I be able to have an impact on any of the subatomic levels while I was, what appeared to be, pure thought or being? Nothing ventured, nothing gained. But I kept tripping on my preconceptions of what it would take to think a change. I couldn't scrunch a feature in concentration. I couldn't scratch a beard or a head. I didn't even feel I could ask anyone any questions—after all, if I were pure consciousness, how could I find or connect with any other conglomeration of the same?

And yet, here I was, philosophizing. Obviously I had capacity to reason, even without the fidgets of a body to make me feel like I was accomplishing something. Maybe this wasn't a futile task. So I spread myself thin, through the solar system we had inhabited, felt the solar winds brushing through the wisps of my thoughts, felt magnetized by the dark matter that penetrated my presence.

I wasn't sure what I was looking for, since I had only ever calculated out the one Higgs particle—and that only to 5 sigma. I couldn't tell what would magnetize one to come to me in my current non-state. And I had a hard time concentrating given the background noise that permeated the area. I had always heard astronomers talk about it as background radiation and white noise, but this was distracting, because it wasn't that random, or lulling. This was more like what people likened to the music of the spheres. It was beautiful, and if anything were going to distract me while I was searching, this would be it: I wanted to let it seep into my being. I wanted to wallow in it. I wanted to let it sweep me away in a flood of emotion and release. Since I couldn't count on being incorporeal without some other random act of violence, I had to turn my back on the artistry of that noise to try to gather other input and ideas.

It felt like the proverbial needle in a haystack. One sub-atomic particle in a multi-verse of particles, and me, formerly a planet, now somehow tied to the physical plane sufficiently that I could be cognizant of it, but not necessarily effective enough to achieve my goal. Certainly this cerebral version of myself had the mental wherewithal to consider problems, and maybe even solve them, but it was hard to imagine an ability to implement anything without access to tools or ways of manipulating matter.

Who knows how long I wafted in that state. I even had some decent ideas for eliminating certain causes of uncertainty. But the music that had subsided to background noise suddenly slapped me in my face—if I had possessed one, anyway, that's what I would imagine it to feel like. What if that music were part of the solution?

Unfortunately for me, that seemed to be my indication of a new transition while I was this diffuse. It was like rushing down train tracks in a dark tunnel, and I was blinded by light as I came out the other end.

Chapter 23

It was akin to a religious experience: being reborn again and again. Never knowing what might direct the path of these jumps, nor knowing how long I might chance to stay in one where-when. This time, I was furry when my head cleared enough to find my bearings. I brought a hand up to my face, and saw monkey-like fingers. Looking around revealed another clearing, not dissimilar to the one in which Sarah and I had married several jumps back, though without the suspended cathedral connected to the ring of trees. I wasn't sure how to define what I was without something reflective, or at least some sort of movement, so stood up and shook myself off. Apparently here, too, I had fallen over. In doing so, I could feel fur rippling in the breeze of my motion, and out of my peripheral vision I noticed a long tail.

Was I some sort of lemur? Man was I in for an interesting ride. I knew a little about these animals—in particular, that ring-tailed lemurs were aggressive around each other. I couldn't tell enough about my physiology, or even the colors of my fur, to be certain of my classification or identification. I did find my toilet-claw, though, and, as if that were some subliminal signal to begin grooming, started picking through the strands of my fur. It was simultaneously satisfying and weird: I was watching my actions through the lens of a human perspective. Contorting to follow the path of an itch (and noting in passing that I was, once again, male), or to flick a louse off, or chew on the next one, seemed both natural and disgusting. Who wants to eat raw bugs? Not me. My survival skills barely qualified me for a snowstorm in Alaska, let alone free-range camping in a completely wild environment.

I wondered if being a lemur meant I was somewhere off the coast of Africa, or if the geology of this planet had been as distinct from my original Earth template as it had been the last time I was a tree-dweller. I was, once again, definitely at home in the heights. My goofy lope, leaping side to side, and reaching for branches to swing myself up higher into the surrounding hardwoods was also comfortable, in that oddly dichotomous way. I wasn't sure where my hindbrain was urging me to go, but it seemed I had a definite destination. Then I realized I was following a scent. It was Sarah—and she was approaching her first heat. I had to race faster to make sure no interloper would find her first to deny my claim. Faster and faster, hand over hand, swinging from tree to tree, deeper into the dense forest, until I could hear her screams.

That wasn't good. Someone else must have found her first, and she was making her displeasure known. Adrenaline pumped through my system and bushed out the fur on my body. Something told me this would be my first mate fight, and the part of me that was human, and valued experience, worried that this did not bode well for the outcome of the upcoming confrontation.

Suddenly I was on top of a whole troop of lemurs. We were definitely all the same species, and I could smell competing scent markers as first one, then another, male stropped each other across the face and chest with their fluffy tails. If I had been Logan, studying this behavior would have been interesting. In the face of the large canine incisors, and the tumbling mass of male bodies between Sarah and me, this was cause for near panic. I couldn't let on my distress. I had to win Sarah; it would be the only way for me to continue making sense of the senselessness of these jumps.

I realized that having a scientific and strategic human viewpoint might be a benefit, as I watched the swirling mass of males below me. Some seemed to forget that the goal was mating rather than fighting; and some found the distraction of fight wounds overwhelmed whatever biological insistence Sarah's scent glands might otherwise have exercised. The fight appeared to be moving away from her—and she was encouraging the distance by moving toward me. If I could just sneak up on her, grab her, and carry her into the trees, we could be mated without the necessity of a fight.

I was gleeful when my maneuver actually worked. It helped that Sarah wanted to go with me; she chittered her disdain for the other males, and expressed her indignation that I hadn't been closer by when full estrous had hit. And don't ask me how I knew that was what she was expressing; I seemed to be getting better at accumulating the cellular knowledge of the being I was inhabiting with each jump. At the same time, I still couldn't tell you what, exactly, the mechanism was that allowed me to keep each of those sets of memories distinct and tied to whatever part of myself was being whirled through this vortex of space-time.

We reached a sturdy V in the thick bole of one of the nearby trees and clung to each other, as our biology dictated the next step in this process. In some ways it was so much less than any other love experience I had shared with any of the previous versions of Sarah.

In other ways, it was distinctly more. I had won her, after all, by the sheer application of my wits—with a little help from her selection of me, as well. We were physically bound as we mated, though that was also a short process, but the emotional ties exploded in whole new ways. I knew I would be able to feel Sarah's location in this wilderness regardless of any obstacles that might be between us. I wondered remotely if Earth's biologists had ever realized the extent of connection between pair-bonded lemurs, and resolved that if I ever got home, I'd look into that field to discreetly share the knowledge that these creatures would sicken and die without both parties being in reasonable proximity to one another.

Sarah's typically soothing presence calmed me down after my wild flight through the woods. I had to wonder why we had been so far apart in the first place. That wasn't the usual result of my shift, and she had been worried about where I was until the moment she smelled my approach. What in the world could I learn from a lemur's perspective that would help me realign with that missing Higgs particle? There would be no lab work. No systematic research documentation. Some insights I'd gained as a planetary being were even confusing to the brain I inhabited now.

Here, I was so focused on scent and sound that visual cues almost fell off my radar. I knew I was looking at that characteristically conical face shape, as Sarah huddled close to me, and I suspected we both wore the same shade of tan or gray fur, but neither of these things mattered as much as the fact that we had merged scents. Sarah smelled like the best part of me, and her presence was necessary for me to feel at home. Her vocalizations had meaning, but so did her silence, and our communication was not limited to just those expressions. We both listened for the drip of raindrops on the forest canopy to hear where there might be a puddle of water. We could hear the insects scratching out their homes in the trees. More importantly, we could feel the air pressure changes when a harrier hawk flew by in search of a meal.

Those almost-attacks were the worst. I knew there was nothing I could do to save Sarah should a hawk take a fancy to her flesh; I also knew I would throw myself into its talons to make sure Sarah would have a chance to escape.

We created a protected nest for ourselves; here again, I used that bit of my human logic that insisted less visibility from overhead would increase our chances for survival. It wasn't anything other lemurs had seen before, but they were quick to learn and apply the logic for themselves.

Once again, I was surprised at the ability to learn from beings I would originally have classified as lesser than myself. We were so very focused on each moment, and the ways our reality reflected back on us, that time became irrelevant. It didn't matter how long or how short Sarah's gestation was going to be. It took the time it took, and we enjoyed every moment of the process. It gave me a whole new perspective on space-time.

Humans were so obsessed with passing time, or saving time, or getting the most out of time that they lost sight of the fact that it was a construct. It didn't have anything to do with the underlying reality of existence. Scientists had learned to account for it as a dimensional cue, since it was a key part of the definition of existence: if you weren't in a particular place at a given time, you could not have been defined as being there. It sounded tautological the first time I heard it, but the logic was sound: the definition of a point couldn't be complete without taking into account the spatial dimension that said: "this thing was here at this time."

Since my time kept looping around on itself, time, as such, had ceased to have much meaning for me. I felt viscerally that a great distance separated me from my original body. Regardless of whether I had names for the months and dimensions I had passed through in the intervening time, I was still a long way from where I had started. My inner parade of experiences added a weight of sadness to me; I missed home and Sarah, even with this Sarah in my arms.

Even more, I missed being human—my kind of human, with food I had grown up with, regular interaction on a non-psi- or non-scent-based level. I missed having a room with four walls, a roof over my head, and the ability to buy rather than forage for my food. Most of all, I missed being able to exercise my scientific expertise. Sure, there were things I had learned that could inform future experiments (if I were lucky enough to ever get home again), but the discipline of documenting theories and findings, and then reporting and sharing my results, were only rare occurrences in this body-hopping exploration of other dimensions.

I worried that the expression "you can never go home again" might be more applicable than usual for me—after all, how would I fit all the knowledge accumulated in all these shifts back into my old circumstances? And who would believe me if I ever told anyone about this wild gallivant through space-time?

On the other hand, since I had confessed to one version of Sarah, it seemed that all versions of Sarah were attuned to these quantum-level changes in me. This one had barely blinked when I had told her I had no idea why I was on the far side of the forest when we should have been together in preparation for her heat. Of course, maybe that was a function of how now-centric we were, in this form, but it also felt like my spirit—or whatever else you want to label it—had dispersed some of its quantum confusion through the cells of the bodies we had touched. All of them seemed to be aware of the changes, and since Sarah had been so intimately tied to them, she knew too.

In the spirit of scientific inquiry, though, I asked Sarah whether she understood I wasn't the me I had been before our mating. She flicked her whiskers at me. "I'm not that me, either."

I almost fell off the branch we were huddled on. "What do you mean?"

"Every time you shift, I do too. I've been with you the whole time."

My jaw dropped in a strangely human expression. "But, how?"

"How am I supposed to know that? You're the one who's supposed to be finding us a way home through that brilliant scientific mind of yours."

"Why didn't you say anything earlier?"

She grinned, a human parody amid the fur. "I figured you knew. Or if you hadn't sorted it out, the fact that you weren't talking about it seemed reason enough to keep my mouth shut."

I felt a real fool. How had I not known that my own Sarah had been with me all this time? I had always immediately recognized her, but what was the mechanism that had us both jumping bodies on a regular basis? And if the phenomenon had captured both of us, how many others were also experiencing this dislocation? It put a whole new spin on some of Richards' actions in recent interactions. Was he growing frustrated at my lack of progress? Was that why he had demolished my planet? Was there a possibility that some of our actions were predestined? Was he always going to be a catalyst for me? I hadn't noticed him since our arrival here; did that mean I was on my own for sorting out our next step?

My ongoing curiosity reassured me once again that I hadn't lost some essential element of my being with all these shifts. I was still blown away by the fact that Sarah had been my Sarah all along. How had she known how to do the things she had done in those other realities? Somehow it was hard for me to trust this confession, coming from a lemur. Weren't they known for causing mischief? I looked at this being, who was my mate here, as in every other reality I had known, and decided that if the universe had enough of a sense of humor to send me zipping through so many different realities, there was probably enough room to play this trick on me too. It was odd, though, that Sarah seemed to have so much easier of a time of making these transitions, and understanding what to do with the different bodies she was shoved into.

But then again, Sarah had always had that creative turn of mind. It had allowed her to adapt to life in Alaska as easily as she had to life in DC, and had allowed her to make use of found objects for her crafts or to learn new crafting styles with equal ease. She was, as always, a remarkable individual. In this adventure, she was content to treat our bouncing journey as an extended honeymoon—and she had no trouble forgiving me for missing our original night as man and wife, since she had now gotten to experience several from wildly different perspectives. "People always ask after you come back from the honeymoon: Do you have any regrets? I will be able to thoroughly, and categorically, deny those. You've taken me on the trip of a lifetime, and proved that it doesn't matter where, or what, we are: we'll always be together, and are, in every way, compatible."

She sighed and snuggled deeper against me. I wasn't sure she understood the magnitude of what we had been experiencing, since it involved so many different realities, and times, and beings. I didn't know if we would ever get back to ourselves. But I wasn't ready to share those worries with her. I figured if she were still OK with us being together (and she hadn't mentioned an awareness of the time factor in our shifts), I had more of a grace period left before I started getting the "I wanna go home" complaint.

Even as I thought that, I knew Sarah was not the childish kind to complain. Even if she might well be sick and tired of this kind of life, she was the kind of loyal and supportive person who would buck up and accept it, since she knew I was in the same boat with her. She had often said that home was wherever I was. I hoped that satisfaction would be sufficient for her as the shifts continued. The more often we were in these animal beings, the less chance I would have to investigate ways of plugging whatever Higgsian leak seemed to be the cause of our current predicament.

Still, we were together, and this Sarah was my Sarah, and we were going to have another child—in another world, through another species, in an unknown, unknowable time. Yet there is always excitement in bringing a new life into the world. The scientific, rational side of myself that delighted in new data points thoroughly enjoyed tracking where and when there was movement in Sarah's belly, and the other ways her body changed. Not that a lemur's body changes all that much, but her scent shifted radically.

Of course, there's no real way to share scent in the written word, other than by vague comparisons. In this case, I couldn't even approximate an analogous smell, but the shift was equivalent to moving from vanilla—bland undertone for a lot of different recipes—to

ginger—spicy overtone that instantly changed the flavor of everything around it.

Unfortunately, for lemurs, the scents of pregnant females were as
alluring as those of non-pregnant ones, so I had to spend a lot of
time defending our space from males who thought that by dint of
assiduous grooming, they might inherit a baby by luring Sarah away
from her mate. There was some very strange politicking going on
along these lines that I never did fully understand, but it made me a
nervous wreck while we were in that dimension.

You could well ask me what a lemur would have to be nervous
about, but first-time parents would be much more in tune with my
mindset than you might think—since I had had the early parenting duties on several other worlds by now. But this was the first as
a lemur, where other lemurs were interested in absconding with
our young one, and where I knew the Sarah who was with me was
the same Sarah I had fallen in love with so long ago. It was almost
as good as having made it to my wedding night with her, and now
reaping the fruit of our love together.

Not having previously been a lemur, nor having had much chance,
interest, or opportunity to learn about them in any prior circumstance, we had no idea what to expect of the birth, nor even how
long Sarah would gestate the baby. So it came as a thrill when, in
the middle of a night, as we lay curled together, Sarah's contractions
started. The birthing was very similar to what it would have been
as a human, with the baby coming out enveloped in its own caul. I
suppose to our human sides, what we did with that, and the after-
birth, once the little girl was independent of Sarah might be considered the height of disgusting. We were following the instinctive
dictates of the biology we were living, and there wasn't any sign of
the recent birth within minutes of Sarah's delivery.

It was all over in an hour. I much preferred that system to the one with the eggs and the incubator, or even the lengthy birthing process human women go through. For once, my nerves steadied, and I felt like I knew exactly what to do. I took down the roofing boughs we had put in place over our nest, after the infant had successfully nursed. We scattered all the nesting materials, disposed of them as best we could, and scampered through the night in search of a new location where our child would be secure from prying eyes, and avaricious uncles or hungry raptors.

It wasn't typical lemur activity, but we weren't typical lemurs. We understood the risks of staying in one place too long, and the long odds that the child we had just brought into the world would survive to adulthood. So we had decided to do everything we could to hide her from the world until she was sufficiently strong to fend for herself. Of course, being naturalized lemurs, that time came faster than you might expect. The little girl we named Petal was wandering independently within a few weeks.

Since she hadn't been exposed to any other lemurs in her short life, we worried Petal might not have coping skills when faced with a band of them, so we tested the waters on how she might be received. We decided I would be the one most likely to come out of an encounter with our kind unscathed, so I sauntered near our old stomping grounds as if I hadn't a care in the world. I was perturbed when I couldn't pick up any recent lemur scent trails.

My plan had been to act as if nothing had changed; the others would smell the female lemurs on me regardless, and we could adjust our reactions based on their response to those scents. With no lemurs to test my new scent on, I had no further plan.

I scampered back to where Sarah and Petal were hidden and chittered my confusion at them. We were all at a loss. Maybe our sudden disappearance had disconcerted the others enough that they had scattered too? Or had there been a new predator on the loose, who had made a big meal out of all of them? The more we speculated, the more concerned we became.

In the end, there was nothing for it but to go chasing off through the forest in search of any sign of our former band-mates. We didn't want to be obvious about our distress, but we also couldn't fail to attract attention, as we went speeding after each other through the branches.

I wasn't even aware that there was a band of inter-species communication until Sarah pulled up beside me with an intense look on her face. Petal was clutching Sarah's back, trembling with the stress we were radiating. I had all but forgotten about the psi skills we had used in our lizard bodies, but Sarah was putting them to good use. She pointed up into the trees, and we saw a large boa constrictor coiled up, digesting enough of a meal to keep it moribund for a week. I was glad it was already more than full, because any of us could just as easily have been dinner, too.

The snake, however, was feeling expansive in its sated state, so had caught Sarah's attention with a sly insinuation that we might do better not to run around as if we had no sense.

I would have spluttered had that been an option in this body. But the snake had a point. We weren't using the brains that had allowed us some unusual innovations, considering we were lemurs.

Sarah asked point blank whether the snake had heard of any unusual experiences relating to lemurs in recent moons. I thought the snake was going to toy with us, but it was surprisingly forthright. "When the moon was half full, and the stars obscured by high, light clouds, the lemurs of this island disappeared."

That put their disappearance only a few days after the birth of our Petal. And what did the snake mean by "of this island"? We weren't on an island, as far as we knew; we were in the midst of a vast forest. But the snake was adamant, this forest was on an island, and it was surprised to see us because all the other lemurs had scampered off. Disappeared. Vanished. The news wasn't any different any way we asked the question. Finally, the snake got annoyed at our hectoring and hissed loudly. We took the hint and left.

Not that we were running away, exactly, but it did take a while before we decided to slow down and forage. Petal had rid herself of her shakes and, in the nature of a curious child, needed to explore a bit on her own. So Sarah and I sat and combed through each other's fur. The grooming was relaxing. We were calm and comfortable in each other's minds. Sarah wondered if the snake, given its very limited range of motion, would consider its territory an island. It sounded a reasonable hypothesis, but my curiosity was aroused. Were we really on an island? Were we really the only lemurs left here?

It wouldn't be that big of a difference for Petal to become a migrant lemur with us, as we set out to explore the limits of our habitat, so Sarah agreed with my suggestion that we treat this as a learning opportunity for the girl. She needed to know how to handle herself in a variety of circumstances anyway, so this would be our way of educating her in this world.

We had a lot of fun. The first few days, it did seem as though the forest was almost deserted. We certainly didn't run into many other species—not even another boa. It was as if all sentient beings around us had shifted into another dimension without us, and we were the last beings in the world. That wasn't entirely the case, and kept it from being eerie, but the lack of population of things like marmosets and sloths and prey animals like tigers and raptors made me wonder if this might be a new phase of the impact of the missing Higgs particle: a strange isolation from those who might otherwise fall within my sphere.

There wasn't any way to test the theory, and as time went on, I wondered when we would next bounce into a new reality. This time, knowing we were together, and had a daughter who wouldn't be following us, our departure loomed in a way it previously hadn't. In the dark of the night, as Petal slept between us, we quietly discussed how we might best equip her for the potential change in personality she might experience from whatever souls would take our places.

It was futile speculation, since we knew it would be some variation of ourselves, but I had no theory to explain our own displacement, let alone what might be replacing me—or us. Over and over I looked at Sarah in wonder that she had managed to follow along so easily all these times. We were still together. It worried me that she had followed me and I had been both unaware of the fact and that it had been possible in the first place. One Higgs particle lost through my experiment should have only affected one person—the experimenter who had lost the particle. In theory, anyway.

I was in a new realm of sub-atomic physics if that one particle had unraveled multiple lives. It began to seem as though string theory might apply, and we were both on the same string. How did that happen? We had seen my parents, and Richards, in several of our incarnations. Did that mean they were on the same string? Were they the same souls we had known in our original dimension? How did that account for the variations in their personalities? And if they weren't on the same string, did that mean there were that many variations on our own personalities? Which looped us back around to concern for Petal. What if the variants of us that showed up after our departure were as sadistic as the Richards in the alternate reality we had visited a few hops back?

There were no parenting manuals for these kinds of questions. How do you tell your child that you may look the same, but your spirit might have changed sufficiently that you really are a different person? How do you know when you should encourage her to leave you behind and seek out her own path? And how do you drill it into her that if any version of you shows up who harms her, she must understand that it was no reflection on our adoration of her, but rather a fluke of physics? Especially when limited to the scent and grooming language of lemurs?

It was a heartbreaking realization that in order to serve her best, we were going to have to wean her off our presence as soon as possible, to avoid any possibility of harm coming to her because of the scientific conundrum that enveloped us. The only mitigating factor was that lemurs mature quickly, and there was abundant forage for her.

Still, we weren't finding evidence of any other lemurs in the vicinity, and we began to consider the boa might have had some knowledge beyond our ken. If that were the case, how do we tap into that knowledge? How could we find a troop of lemurs with which to leave Petal? And if we were suddenly stranded on an island with no other lemurs, how would Petal manage in the future? Lemurs were social beasts, and she would need others as she grew older, even if we were trying to teach her to be independent of us earlier than we would have liked.

When we reached a shoreline that appeared to face an ocean, we decided this wasn't enough data to confirm everything the boa had told us. It did seem likely it had had some insight that might help us help Petal. After all, islands don't typically exist in the middle of an ocean without some surrounding chain of other islands in reasonable vicinity. So we traveled northward along the coastline, within sight of the ocean, but under cover of the forest.

Several days of travel brought us to a point I assumed might be the furthest tip of the island. Unfortunately, we still hadn't seen evidence of any nearby landmass. It was worrying. Several days' travel ought to have revealed some further information. It was fair, now, to assume this was, indeed, an island, but that would not help us, or Petal. We needed to find a land bridge that would take her to more of our kind.

On top of which, each day's travel brought us closer to the likelihood of side-stepping into a new dimension, so there was a looming deadline adding to our tension.

There was nothing for it but to continue to explore. We decided to track the tides to be able to determine whether time of day had an impact on the visibility, or availability, of additional landmasses. This slowed us down.

Discovering a new cove was worst. We had in front of us what to human-conditioned eyes would be ideal: A stretch of fine sand and clear skies. We could even get out to the point and watch Petal explore the coastal caves as if they were trees of stone. But each time hours passed and the waters receded and we discovered still more water I would grind my teeth at the futility of our search. We weren't going to be around long enough to discover anything useful for Petal.

She was blithely unconcerned about our worries. Maybe it was an effect of her youth, but she didn't seem to have a care in the world. She repeatedly said that it didn't matter to her whether we ever found any others of our kind—she was content to wander with us… whether we were who we were now, or we were some other version of ourselves.

I hoped all the soul-swapping confusion hadn't landed us with a simple child who couldn't comprehend the significance of what we were telling her. But then, I supposed most adults would have a hard time sorting out the details of what we had experienced. In fact, I knew only some of the scope of the problem, and felt over-whelmed by my inability to know where to even begin addressing it.

I was all over the map, and worrying more every day. We hadn't found a solution to Petal's impending parentlessness, and I didn't have access to any tools, materials, or technology that might help me continue to prod the sub-atomic world in the hopes it would rearrange back to its original character.

Despite my worries, my life had never been better. Tropical island, wife and child in tow, no pressure to perform, conform, or other-wise respond to anything other than internal prompts went a long way to lull me into a false sense of tranquility. A whole moon passed this way, waxing and waning while we traveled the coastline. At the dark of the moon, we finally found the land bridge we had been looking for; I suppose had we headed South in the first place, we would have found it sooner. I was just glad it existed at all. I hoped it was the explanation for where the other lemurs had disappeared.

We decided to walk the bridge at the next low tide, mid-morning. It meant we forced Petal to get up and get moving at a time she normally would have been sound asleep. She was cranky and slow to get moving.

The land bridge was considerably longer than I had anticipated. In fact, it was long enough that I wondered whether we would make it to the other side before the tide turned—or before Petal expired of the hunger she was complaining about. Were we just lemmings in this trek? Maybe the reason there were no more lemurs on the island was that they had all been lured by some false promise to walk onto an unreliable passage, then been wiped away by the incoming tide. I was a bit of a pessimist; but who could blame me, after the calamity I had visited on myself and Sarah with that misbegotten Higgs particle experiment?

In fact, the tide was lapping at our feet rather compellingly before we saw our destination. We beheld another large, lush island. What in the world could have drawn off the entire population of lemurs to a location they couldn't even see? Lemurs weren't generally known for having prophets, or listening to outsiders, so this motivation seemed sinister to me. Somebody had to have convinced them to move in a direction they had neither anticipated, nor would likely have gone without the enticement of someone they trusted.

Richards' name whispered through my brain. He had lost Sarah in the odd mating ritual we had enacted at the onset of this visit. He had never before shown any interest in her as a mate in her previous forms. But was he still working to prod me into furthering my work? If so, how did he think a species-specific migration that had never before happened was going to motivate me—when I didn't have the tools to act on any insights that impetus might lend me?

We had to carry Petal the last hundred yards, and I worried our lemur bodies would be weighted down with waterlogged fur that would drown us. We managed to drag our bedraggled selves onto the shore of the new island in the early afternoon. Panting with the effort, we stretched out on the beach. I felt the sun on my fur and laid back to dry out, despite how unprotected that position was.

While we basked, I again contemplated Richards' motivation. He had displayed the widest range of characteristics of any of the recurring characters in my multiverse drama. Did that mean I was seeing him differently through different perceptual lenses, or did that mean he was an unpredictable soul who hadn't sorted out his own meaning, and method for learning and growing? Either way, it made him dangerous.

As if the thought conjured the man, we became aware that there were eyes on us. Not just one set, but hundreds. Hungry eyes: predators' eyes. We were exposed on the beach with our little girl, and had no idea how we were going to save ourselves let alone our offspring. Then the tingles started. I couldn't stand it: I stood up and yowled as if that would keep me in my body long enough to defend this iteration of my family. Sarah must have sensed what I was trying to do, for she stood as well. Petal, however, remained innocent, gently letting sand sift through her fingers and using her toilet claw to pick at the sand that had matted her tail. It didn't keep us in those bodies any longer than any previous herald of a transition had done, but at least I marked the passage with protest.

Chapter 24

Maybe it was my vocalization in the early part of the transition, but I settled in to my new vehicle as smoothly as any time since this had begun. Or had my spirit come to grips with the process and started making it easier on me? Who could know? I was grateful for the reprieve from additional dizziness. Unfortunately, none of that could stop the hammer of grief from falling. For all I knew, vicious predators had overrun Petal. I had failed her.

I could sense Sarah nearby, and strained to understand my environment.

It wasn't anything like any other place or time I had been in this madcap jaunt. I thought I was in some sort of liquid environment again, but didn't see any way of distinguishing portions of myself to confirm the background. And the other beings nearby, while indubitably individuals, were not in an immediately recognizable form. I wondered what I had blundered into this time, when I felt the force of a strange tide moving me. That pretty well settled the question of whether I was in a liquid. I still couldn't tell exactly what I was. It was disturbing to know I was incarnate again, but without any sense of what my body made me.

I was desperate to pursue my studies, but knew I would never manage that without hands to manipulate materials or feet to get me to a work bench. I couldn't find either of those necessary pieces.

Another blob showed up, and I saw an amorphous pseudopod elongate in front of me. It was translucent and jelly-like and reminded me of nothing so much as slime. It was part of me. Disgusting. I was an amoeba. How could I manage anything as a single-celled organism? As far as my limited biology recollections yielded, this life form didn't even reproduce genitally. I'd managed to have children in every other variation on my life; I took it for granted that would be part of my ongoing adventure.

Particularly now that I had gotten more of a handle on the parent-child bond and needed affirmation that there could be someone like Petal in every one of the multiverses we had or would visit. I knew there would be no replacing the uniqueness that Petal had been as a lemur, but since I knew Sarah and I to also be unique, but represented in untold multiples throughout the multiverse, I felt it my duty to ensure that Petal had similar representation. How in the world would I manage that without Sarah's input? And where was Sarah?

I spent a frantic few moments trying to sort out the mechanics of frenzied motion in this new form, before I managed forward movement. The challenge of being an amoeba was the whole non-structured thing: movement was more osmotic than intentional, and distance felt like an insurmountable problem. I wasn't sure if there were some kind of sensory or communication system as I started out—then remembered that it had taken me some time to integrate those in my previous bodies too. When I did, the skill came with time and focus.

I decided the whole movement thing was overrated until I could determine whether there was a communication channel that might help me locate Sarah. I scared myself with the thought that maybe this time we were both here, but she was not an amoeba. What if she were the organism in which I, the amoeba, lived? How would we communicate then? I had to have a sense of her presence in order to feel comfortable with additional action; without that, I wouldn't know if I were harming her with my choices.

Concentrating while a single-celled organism was a challenge. I kept feeling like I should have a brain to manage thoughts, but that science-text image of an amoeba ruled out that possibility. So my thoughts bounced through my being in an uncoordinated mass, moving from Sarah to Petal to experiments to food to … wait: Food? Why was that even an issue now? I had noticed in my motion that I could absorb nutrients. How did that not sate my need for feeding?

In any case, that was all beside the point: Sarah had to be my priority. Then Petal. Then getting home. But how could I do any of those things without a brain? I had so much more empathy with the Scarecrow from the *Wizard of Oz*—and noticed that once again I was spinning through topics with all the sense of a headless chicken. This was a disaster. I didn't even have the mechanism of "deep breaths" to help clear my head. In fact: what head?

My freak-out was spiraling out of control, and I couldn't calm down enough to talk myself out of the mess. I felt a gentle nudge. I wanted to turn and see what had managed that kind of action, but the idea of orientation was based on my acculturation as a human.

An amoeba doesn't orient that way. An amoeba just reaches out a pseudopod.

There was Sarah. How do you know it's you when you're an amoeba? And how do you know it's Sarah when it's an amoeba? It's all the same strange syncretistic question. There is no knowing without a sense of an individual. Amoebas are so similar, I had no idea what it would take to solidify my identification without some method of communication.

How was it that Sarah was plastic enough that she could master these body doubles so much more quickly than I? I had always known her to be an amazingly creative individual—it was one of the things I loved about her—but figuring out how to manipulate the basic element of ectoplasmic goo took my esteem to a whole new level.

I sensed her distant laughter, and wondered how she had managed that. Apparently there was, indeed, a communication channel in this form. Now the question was: how do I access it? I stretched out another pseudopod in what I hoped was her direction. I would normally have laughed about the blind leading the blind, but I knew I must have had some sense of my surroundings to be able to identify that I was floating in liquid. Could I add to my analysis? There were light and dark fields, and I seemed to have oriented toward the light. That awareness helped me orient toward Sarah as well: she was the blob next to me, and had also stretched out a pseudopod. If we had been human, I would have said we were holding hands.

I couldn't feel Sarah's hand now, but I could feel her thoughts. I understood her amusement at this predicament, and wished I could adopt a similarly carefree attitude. But I felt responsible for how far off kilter our world had spun and didn't like to think I had let her down, or led her astray. She seemed able to pluck out the threads of my morose attitude and understand me, while I was still floundering with the concept of communication between single-celled beings.

She arranged her pseudopods around me in a mimic of a human hug. If I could have cried, I would. I longed to be human and feel her arms around me for real.

If someone at home had told me single-celled beings are emotional, and their emotions affect them like they do humans, I would have scoffed. How could depression suppress an immune system in something so self-contained? My depression, however, threatened my life. The more I cringed about how badly I had underestimated my initial tests, the more I folded in on myself and shrunk. How can a single-celled being shrink? Another Koan for an empiricist to study. I didn't think about it, even as I felt the feverish action of not only Sarah but other amoebas around me, as they reached out their pseudopods and tried to pluck at my cellular membranes. I didn't even think about it as I noticed a painful squeezing sensation.

Then I realized I wasn't an amoeba anymore. I saw a pin-prick of goo. A mass of mourning amoebas surrounded the remains of my amoeba body. I hadn't intended to self-annihilate. It seems I had blotted myself out under the weight of my depression. A sobering thought, that. And here I was, back to wondering what it was that was left of me that could consider any of these things. How was I now different—more *me*—than I had been as an amoeba? How did I know that the amoeba who was now fighting its own compression tendency was Sarah? What was it that led to self-identification when there truly were no features associated with an individual?

I had to shake myself—that was Sarah down there. She had just witnessed me dying in her grasp, and she was struggling not to be strangled by her grief. Part of me was horrified at the thought that I could contribute further to the house of horrors her life had become. Another, very small part of me, hoped she would follow me again, so I could hear her counsel, and understand what it was about her that allowed her such easy access to the emotions, sensations, and mechanics of the diverse collection of beings we had now inhabited together. I spent so much time trying to figure out what I was, I missed out on key information along the lines of: 'ware the depression, in some bodies it will kill you.

Still, I was glad not to be constrained to thoughts obsessively focused on the limitations of being a single-celled organism. That brought me up short: If I were now pure spirit, didn't that mean I was now a no-celled organism? Why wouldn't it bother me that I could think, and reason, and deduce in this state when those faculties had first rebelled, and then literally imploded, in my previous state? I stumped myself. Sarah was still shrinking before my enthralled perception. Now, she too had the innumerable pseudopods reaching out to stroke her cellular surface. I suspected she was close to the end. I moved closer, intent on catching her to me before her spirit dissipated in front of me.

She seemed to sense my presence. How would you know, though, if an amoeba were to look in your direction? Her knowledge did nothing to steady her in that body; if anything, she burst forth from her shell much more quickly in her effort to reach me once more.

Chapter 25

Here again, it was peculiar in hindsight to know that I had not only, technically, committed suicide, but had also been the motivating factor in Sarah's self-annihilation. I had always considered that the path of the weak-minded; those who wouldn't accept their gifts, or their importance to those around them, discredited themselves with that action. Yet here, because we were such insignificant beings, reverting to a non-celled state seemed absolutely preferable. What did it say about me that I would consistently identify a hierarchy of beings and place humans at the top of the pile, when my circumstances had proved repeatedly that life wasn't that simple? There were bodies gifted with senses I would never own in human form. And there were insights I never would have gained without the knowledge harvested from other selves.

At that moment, though, I was too happy to have yet another reunion with Sarah to be distracted by those abstractions. I was still frustrated not to be able to gather her into my arms and stroke the silky auburn hair of her original self. I was upset I couldn't gaze into her eyes and caress the soft skin behind her ears. But now, at least, we could communicate. Sarah was a flash of lightening, a stroke of genius, swirling around me.

Here, at least, I could feel every energetic connection we had ever forged as a spiking wavelength that reminded me of goosebumps. And here, we were so intimately connected that our thoughts began and ended in each other, making it difficult to distinguish between us.

Our sparkling connection grew fizzy and it seemed to generate—or maybe illuminate—other presences around us. Had I been oblivious in my prior lack-of-body state that I had missed a similar phenomenon? I wondered what these beings were that had no body, and were congregating around the energetic flames of our joy. Here, at least, I seemed to have access to some answers. Sarah's effervescence highlighted the connections amongst us all, and I finally had evidence of some sort of angelic beings. There were no wings on any of them, but they were focused on delivering a specific message—thus hearkening back to the original definition of the Greek word: messenger.

"You've unraveled yourself and your world, and the longer you stay away from it, the more damage you do to the worlds around you," thrummed from all of them at various frequencies.

"I know this is bad, and finding out that Sarah had been pulled into the displacement only recently reinforced my sense of impending disaster. But until I can get someplace where I have a body and a lab, I don't even know how to test a theory about putting reality back together again," I complained.

"You needed the different perspectives to be able to put the puzzle back together, but you've been ignoring the most important lessons."

Suitably chastised, I asked, "Would it be possible for an intercession to help me back into a body where I can at least see whether I could track down the missing Higgs particle?"

There was utter stillness around me. I didn't know whether they had disappeared to indicate their disgust or to carry my message forward. I also didn't know if their few words indicated there was a higher power at play that was pushing me into such multifarious conditions. It had seemed so random at the time. I looked again for Sarah. Maybe she would have some insight for me.

She was subdued too, at the thought that we might have neglected some important aspect of learning. I remembered my previous passage through pure-spirit state, and my speculation about the necessity of an observerless observer, thereby mitigating the Schroedinger's cat phenomenon impacting sub-atomic particles. It occurred to me that the fact that the messengers hadn't censured me about the suicide bit could be significant. Had they validated my need to be pure spirit to resolve the conundrum?

Sarah perked up at the direction of my thoughts. She had been raised an observant Catholic, so the thought she might be anathema in any state bothered her profoundly. She had been the one to declare our earth-bound wedding to be out of bounds of the church, and yet, many hops through alternate realities later, she battled the irony of struggling against the imprinting of her childhood. It seemed an insight that might speak to the nature of our core beings. How much were we impacted by our various life episodes; how much of those events carried forward with us into our spiritual selves?

From my perspective, the lessons from being a four-fingered mostly human, to being an amphibian, to being a lemur, to being an amoeba all seemed crisply accessible. What thread was it that held each of those trials together? Sarah was drawn deeper into my thinking as I followed the logic. She contributed: "I always knew I was me, just in a different aspect. It was like an archetype of me that could sustain characteristics I embraced."

I pursued the concept of a generic version of myself. I had always thought of generic as being bland, but this seemed to point to a super-set of energies. Maybe our souls were an even finer representation of the sub-atomic world? Maybe we were inextricably tied to the Dark Matter science had not yet been able to quantify? Certainly our ability to interact in the disembodied state felt a strange combination of energetic and materialistic.

What if I had stumbled onto the discovery of a soul particle—that irreducible element that made each of us unique, and presented the possibility of a range of particulars within a given life's context? It was a thrilling potential. But it would open up a raging debate in my home context: science had long derided the God-particle, and this was dangerously close to that postulate. What would I need to do to prove the theory?

Sarah and I drifted together for a time, enjoying the simple pleasure of each other's presence, with no sense of the urgency a body and its needs can impose. I had no idea how long we might be granted this interlude, but I was determined to enjoy it as fully as possible. It was absolutely a different perspective on the essential Sarah: her energy was bright and bubbly in a way I wouldn't have categorized from my original knowledge of her. I suspected she was learning new things about me too, but didn't want to hear what she might say about my density—a theme carried over from her teasing from our original selves.

Still, we hashed through our memories of the lives we had left behind. She tweaked my metaphoric nose that while I had been able to distinguish her for herself, I had always doubted that she might be the same person I had known from home. I had to defend myself by sharing the scientific improbability that both of us might be living through the same anomaly. The odds against it were astronomical—unless there were a god force that most scientists I knew would ridicule as impossible to prove.

Sarah worried that the messengers who had come to us might also mean we were in danger of failing in our mission to re-weave our realities. I heard the related concern that she might be damned if we failed. I pointed out that this was entirely my mess—I still had no idea why she was along for the ride. I was thrilled to be able to see her on a regular basis, I would do everything I could to make sure her immortal self suffered no negative consequences of my actions.

That made her laugh. "We're each only responsible for our own actions. I've always chosen to be with you. Whatever path you're on will naturally reflect on me, and I hope my influence will reflect on you too."

That was deeper than I had considered.

"What if this in-between-bodies state is the only way we plug the hole that led to the unraveling we're in trouble for?"

"You're thinking of Schroedinger's cat, right?"

Sarah had always surprised me with her grasp of such a wide range of subjects. You would never think that someone as obsessed with crafting and weaving, and the natural world, would even have access to that kind of casual interpretation. You would be sadly underestimating my Sarah, then.

"Right. I think I goofed by detaching a Higgs boson in a facility where so many other secret tests were being conducted, and I didn't take into account the possibility that quantum entanglement might play a deeper role than my colleagues thought." I was getting into some dangerous areas by admitting that I knew of other top-secret trials, but in this state, it would also be hard not to share such details.

"But if I take off from what you were saying about archetypal selves, and could suggest that quantum entanglements are a micro reflection of the macro entanglement of a relationship, maybe we could use our relationship as a test bed for fixing that hole," I continued.

Sarah indicated assent with what would have been a head-bob, had she been human. And it reminded me that in this disembodied form we could be both wave and particle selves—possibly another clue in the mystery of re-integrating what I had broken. The real question, though, was how to test our relationship. We hadn't been in control of any of the dimensional bounces we'd gone through so far. We could at least test how our energies interacted in this space, to see whether we could sense anything on the subatomic level.

This was the kind of pure science that had always thrilled me. I could get obsessive about how each element interacted with the next, and track down every last smidgen of data. We weren't ourselves so much as a sub-quantum collection of some kind of energy I had never seen before. If we coalesced ourselves, we could push quantum chain reactions depending on what kinds of thoughts we sent to each other. This was fun—and potentially useful. It felt like we might be working toward a solution to reweave ourselves into our original reality.

I was positive we were on the right track. Sarah laughed at my enthusiasm but was right there with me. It felt like we should be glowing in the classic "gone nuclear" depictions from old cartoons. So, somehow, we did. I couldn't call it bioluminescence, because we had no biology in this form, but it reminded me a lot of the Förster resonance energy transfer equations and their undetectable virtual photon transfers. That was all in the realm of a violation of the conservation of energy and momentum laws, too. Yet it was measurable and verifiable regardless. It was a whole new avenue of interest to pursue. Maybe our soul particles were at the same level as the virtual photons, and that was why we could interact with and modify each other without actually having physical bodies to convey those touches. I wondered if that was also the source of the chemistry poets so often struggled to define: a sub-quantum entanglement that didn't even have a language in scientific literature.

The more we whipped each other up in a frenzy of anticipation over the next energetic level we might find together, the more we intensified that sense of glowing, and the more I anticipated returning to our original, normal state. It was a captivating process. And it ended abruptly when I discovered I was in a human body again.

Chapter 26

Had we succeeded? Were we back to normal? As my eyes acclimated to perception again, I found I was in a lecture hall where an uncomfortable silence was growing. I glanced left and right and discovered people looking at me. I looked up, and an older man in a tweed sport coat tapped his fingers against his lectern as his eyes sought to bore a hole in my head. I must've missed something.

"Mr. Inman, could you please answer the question, since you have seen fit to disrupt class with your outburst?"

Apparently I was me again, but I didn't know this man. This class didn't resemble any that I had ever previously participated in, and I had no other recourse than, "I'm sorry for the trouble, Sir."

He snorted at me, and a wave of titters rolled over my nervous classmates as the man proceeded with his lecture. It sounded like some kind of sociology, which wasn't something I had ever studied before, or been interested in, so I thought I would be drawn into the new subject. Instead, my mind wandered again: how had Sarah and I precipitated this jolt into a new body?

My only guess related to the amped-up energy we had produced with our back and forth energetic whipsaw. Was there a certain frequency we had to reach to put the change in motion? Of course, I hadn't had a body to feel the characteristic tingles, or sense the change in vision that had usually preceded my shifts, but maybe those were because of the increased sub-quantum-level energetic ramp up. It was an interesting line of thought. I jumped as the bell signaled the end of the class.

I stood slowly, to make sure I really was in a human body and wouldn't topple over from the change. All the students had left by the time I gathered up my belongings and began shuffling toward the door.

"Mr. Inman?"

I jerked my head around and saw the professor. "Yes?"

"Your outburst of nonsense words was uncharacteristic and inappropriate. Do you want to explain yourself?"

I looked at him blankly. This body had produced nonsense words just prior to the change-over? Did that mean the outgoing portion of myself had had some sense of the move in the same way I did? Or was that a different effect of the passage through space-time? I stuttered as I realized I didn't even know this man's name—or the proper etiquette in this circumstance for addressing him. I fell back on the respectful address required at my original alma mater: "Professor, I'm not sure what happened there. Maybe a waking dream?"

I trailed off in the hopes that he would dismiss me and be done with the conversation; I needed to find out what had happened to Sarah with this latest bounce.

"Why would you have been falling asleep in class that way? My daughter hasn't been keeping you up with inappropriate contact, has she?" His eyes crinkled at the corners as he spoke.

His small clue shook me, and I ventured to respond, "Oh no, sir. Sarah's great!"

He looked puzzled, and I had the sinking sensation that maybe in this space-time, for the first time ever, anywhere, we might not be together that way. But his proceeding sentence absolved me of that worry: "Son. I thought we had gotten over the formalism. When we're alone you can call me Clark."

He waved his hand at the patently empty hall and smirked, letting its state underline his statement. I gave him a sheepish look. "I'm sorry. It takes some getting used to."

He laughed. "The wedding is only a week away and there are still a lot of final details to review. In fact, Sarah and Margaret were hoping you'd come over after class to have supper with us, and talk a little more."

I took it that in this area of space-time Clark and Margaret were in the roles of Sarah's parents. It was odd that my name hadn't changed—and this man, Clark, apparently still recognized me for myself—but Sarah's parents' names had. I was leery about testing their last name on my lips until I had some further clues about the lay of the land.

Helping me do just that, Clark steered me out the door and said, "I just need to swing by my office to pick up some essays I need to finish grading tonight."

He said it with a strange wink and nod. Was he letting me in on a secret? Maybe he didn't like the wedding planning and this was his out?

I huffed a small laugh, since that seemed to be called for, and re-played our conversation. Was I making sense to this man who was to be my father-in-law? Given how poor my acting skills had been in my one attempt at participating in a play in junior high school, I had to assume even on different planes I was more consistent than anyone else I knew.

Or maybe that was because I was the pivot for all the transitions so operated as the point of logical continuation. It would be another thing to ponder.

We paused at the end of the hallway, and Clark turned toward a door, helpfully labeled Dr. Clarkson. What a ridiculous name com-bination; yet I couldn't laugh. I had to work hard not to choke on the snorts that were coming close to offending my future father-in-law. I tried to cover it with a fake coughing fit, but Clark raised an eyebrow at me.

Over my watering eyes, I pulled off the best nonchalant shoulder-shrug I could manage, and spluttered "it's been one of those days."

Clark seemed to be in a remarkably understanding mood for all my disruptions, and I could see where Sarah had gained some of her phlegmatic equilibrium. He fumbled with his keys for a minute before opening the door to a classically disorganized office. There were papers on the verge of toppling, and books on every available surface, but he skated between them with the ease of much practice. He made a quick grab for a stack of blue books piled on what must have been his in box. I stayed well back from the disaster zone for fear of upsetting some element of this disorganization. He eyed me as he came back through the door and snorted. "You never get over that, do you?"

I put on my most convincing innocent look and shrugged again.

He laughed and cuffed my upper arm. "Eh. We all have our own systems, and it's a live and let live world out there, so you can keep your sparkling clean lab bench and alphabetized files, and I'll enjoy having everything I need at fingertips' reach."

This time I laughed. Describing that chaos as allowing him to have everything at fingertips' reach was a stretch by even the most generous account. We walked in companionable silence back along the hall, down a massive stone staircase, and out into a blustery, cold winter's day. This threw me for another loop. Always before, our wedding had been in June. I couldn't remember the last time I had gotten to stay somewhere long enough to shiver through a winter. It was disconcerting.

Clark strode briskly ahead, while I stood still for a moment and felt my teeth start to chatter. What kind of fool was I not to have noticed winter gear piled into my case? Clark noticed he was walking alone, and turned around to see where I was. My numb fingers fumbled at the latch on the closure tab to my satchel. I retrieved my scarf and gloves. Clark shook his head and held out his hand to take possession of that encumbrance while I tried to warm up with the belated additions to my attire.

I noticed he only had on his sport coat. Wasn't he cold?

When I took back my bag, he said, "I'll never understand how you can be so thin-skinned. The house is only two blocks away, so you should survive long enough to see the girls again."

I shook my head and forbore to mention anything about sub-quantum energetic interactions, or the dangers of dimensional shifting. After all, I couldn't be sure that had any impact on my perception of this temperature—and there was no way of knowing whether my spirit particles had any impact on temperature acclimation either. Certainly, you wouldn't have thought that could be the case, given how ephemeral those elements seemed to be. Did the lack of acclimation have anything to do with the fact that I hadn't lived through anything akin to true winter in what might have amounted to years?

That thought jolted me as much as any previous one: I had lived many months in each incarnation, and I had lived at least half a dozen lives. That meant, by my old reckoning, I had been gone years. It made me feel old to imagine how much time had passed in my original timeline.

Given how time looped around, it was likely I could end up back where I had started—a new spin on immortality if I looked at it another from another perspective. I wasn't sure I appreciated that possibility as much as the old questers in search of the fountain of the waters of life. What was the point of all of these events without an underlying order to the through-line of a lifetime?

Clark elbowed me again, to draw my attention to the street crossing we had reached. "You're sunk in a lot of deep thoughts today. Pull yourself out of it, buddy, or Sarah and Margaret will have something to say about it. You know how they get when they have that kind of project between their teeth—you wouldn't want to distract them from wedding preparations."

We laughed again. I had to admit mine was a tad forced, but somehow this afternoon's ruminations reminded me of one of those funhouse halls of mirrors—infinite in every direction I looked, and no comfort that there might be an end to the madness.

Across the street, I looked up to see a classically half-timbered home with a wide veranda gracing the whole front. This seemed to be where we were headed, and I was thankful to again be seeing things that compared favorably with the life I had left behind. I was so focused on counting windows, and rail spindles, and walkway slates that Clark had to elbow me again to get me to look up. Sarah stood in the doorway.

She looked nothing like I'd ever seen her previously: Her hair was a blond cascade of ringlets that tumbled down over her shoulders and back, and highlighted high cheekbones. Her blue eyes registered a charming welcome as I stared at her in wonder.

Clark sighed again, and muttered something about letting the lovebirds warm each other up, before hustling into the house and leaving us in the entryway. I reached for Sarah's hands before I remembered that I was still bundled in gloves and scarf. I hastily removed them before engulfing her in a fierce embrace.

"I thought I had lost you this time."

Sarah looked up at me. She glanced back over her shoulder, reached up to grab my cropped hair, and planted a heavy kiss on my lips. She whispered, "They're conservative here. We're going to be facing more supervision than we're used to for this week. My parents seem to be other people, and we seem to be in a completely different hemisphere, since it's June and we're in early winter."

A throat-clearing noise emanated from behind Sarah. I looked up to see a woman, who bore a passing resemblance to this version of Sarah, standing at the other end of the foyer. With hands on her hips, she was doing her best to appear stern, but there was a small smile playing about her lips. "I can't leave you two alone for a moment, can I? What was Clark thinking?"

She tut-tutted as she strode over to divest me of my outerwear and satchel, and urged us into what could only be described as a parlor. It seemed that this version of June 2012 was back to less technology, and fewer modern inclinations. What possibility would I have of continuing my research?

I was dazed at how quickly events moved each time I made a new jump. Here again, Sarah was ahead of me on the learning curve and seemed to have had no problems with adjusting to new cultural mores, regardless of what her soul-particle-based inclinations might otherwise have been. It was comforting to feel like even though I was rootless in time and space, I still had a home with her.

In this case, that turned out to be more literally true than I might have anticipated. Plans were well underway to convert part of the house into an apartment for the two of us to occupy once the nuptials were past. In fact, we were to discuss some of the unfinished plans that evening.

In this community, it seemed that the tradition was for the bride's parents to provide the first home for their daughter and her new spouse. In the days before the wedding, they would open their doors to visitors to show off the new space. The visitors then had the interesting task of choosing a space they would furnish as their gift to the newlyweds. I could appreciate the practicality and the spirit of mutual support, but it seemed like much too much to count on from mere neighbors. I had never lived in a "traditional" human neighborhood before that would open its arms this way.

It did remind me of my time as a tree-dwelling humanoid, though.

Sarah managed to hold my hand, discretely, behind the bustle of her old-fashioned, floor-length gown, while her mother launched into a full accounting of the various comings and goings and the types of commitments town members had offered us during the previous few days.

From that statement, I inferred I had been lucky to be invited over again so soon after an earlier visit.

The apartment itself was charming—again, in an old-fashioned way. Wood cladding adorned the walls and ceiling and the mantles and doorframes were of carved timber. It reminded me of a Swiss chalet. The faint scents of cedar and oak overlaid the whole tour. I could see us being comfortable living here, regardless of how close we would be living to her parents. They both seemed happy with our match and were taking all the small, supportive steps that helped me know they approved of our intent to marry.

The tour was over soon enough, and we sat down to a new sym-phony of scents. I smelled lamb and mint jelly and roasted potatoes, and saw those represented only a small selection of the dishes spread out across the table. A real meal! I couldn't remember the last time I had seen this kind of welcome wagon rolled out for me. Certainly not with food I would call delicacies in any reality.

It appeared that Sarah's family was quite well off. A young woman, in the starched uniform of some kind of paid help, curtsied in the doorway and said the staff was ready to serve the meal.

As soon as the four of us were seated, two staffers came in and whisked away the dishes that had been so beautifully arrayed on the table. I guess they were eye-appetizers priming our salivary glands for the real thing. The first options were from an olive trough, where the strangely shaped implement to spear individual fruits poked uncomfortably into my palm. I felt like a bumpkin as I fumbled a few onto the small plate in front of me, and elected to only take a few so that I wouldn't hold up the process any longer than I already had.

Sarah, naturally, had sorted out the secret to handling the implement, and skillfully transported a small pile onto her plate. While her father was doling out his portion Sarah ducked her head and winked at me. This was the teasing I remembered, and cherished. She could make even a formal, eight-course meal enjoyable.

I'm not sure what all we ate that night, but there were soups and salads at strange intervals. We even had a palate-cleansing sorbet before the lamb course. It felt out of order to me, but then, the most courses I had ever experienced was the standard hors d'oeuvres, meal, and dessert, so what would I know? And how would I live in a household where this level of eating seemed to be the norm?

Clark and Margaret seemed immune to the pampering, and were just cordial when it came to their instructions to the servers. I was glad that the servers had sense enough to keep each portion small, so I wasn't unpleasantly stuffed by the time we received our coffees.

As I had surmised back at the University, Clark soon made his apologies, claiming work obligations, and students who were awaiting feedback on their essays with bated breath. I almost laughed inappropriately, and Clark shot me a warning look underneath beetled eyebrows. "Son, you should ask Sarah and Margaret to take better care of you. You've had a sneaky cough all afternoon—and you were out in the cold without your coat."

I gaped at the man; that was subtle revenge. After all, he hadn't worn any kind of greatcoat himself. Sarah immediately stood up and used her father's words as a pretense to put her hands on my forehead and face. It was more of a caress than her mother knew, but she put a docile face on it with her words: "He doesn't feel feverish to me. But maybe he should stay in the guest suite tonight, to avoid aggravating the tickle into a full-blown cold. We certainly wouldn't want that with the wedding only days away."

Margaret squinted first at Sarah, then at me. I wasn't sure she would go for the suggestion, but she sighed and said, "Well, it's not like the old days, for sure. But everyone knows you're engaged and you've been chaste so far. And we really don't need the groom under the weather with a nasty winter grippe on the eve of the nuptials."

She called for Hester and bustled off to sort out the logistics. This was like being thrown into one of those historical romance novels Sarah used to chortle over with me, with all the formal rules and clothes. I wasn't sure I liked it—except for the fact that I was supposed to be romancing Sarah. She let her fingers wander over my scalp in a gentle massage, and I figured I could learn to tolerate anything. After all, she must be wrapped up in layers of corsets and other underthings, given the tone of all our other interactions here so far.

Corsets. Yikes! I wished I had paid a little more attention to those books.

As usual, Sarah had quickly divined the nature of my thoughts (though, likely, the bulge at my crotch spoke for those without the need for actual words). She leaned in and whispered, "I have a lady's maid. I'll make sure I'm only in a nightie and robe when I come to you. I can't wait to be in your arms again."

I shushed her more urgently than was necessary. But if she kept talking that way, I would embarrass myself at the dining room table, and her mother would have cause for significantly more concern about my overnight visit. We were so close to the goal of being together, I didn't want to chance anything messing up it up.

I took a quick gulp of water and coughed in earnest when Margaret bustled back into the room while Sarah was still playing with the hair at the back of my neck. Sarah's indelicate thwack between my shoulder blades helped settle me down again, but her mother's was not a look I wanted to face again any time soon. I wondered how long we were going to be required to live under Sarah's parents' roof. And then I decided it didn't matter, since the likelihood was that we would have moved on again before that became an issue.

Margaret cleared her throat and said, "The suite is being set to rights as we speak. Why don't we return to the parlor to review the seating chart. And you can update us on your family's travel plans and whether you've had any additional RSVPs to the invitations."

This was my day for blank looks. I had no idea how I was going to get around that answer, unless I faked more coughing to get myself to bed sooner rather than later. I shot a desperate look at Sarah, hoping she might have a clue for me. She moved her shoulders in a micro-shrug that indicated she didn't know either, and responded to her mother. "That was such a big meal. Why don't we play a round of cards to let it settle, and see whether Mark's cough settles down."

That, I could do. And actually look forward to: I had been part of a Sheepshead team in college, and we had brought home the championship twice while I was in the group, so I was proud of my card sharping abilities—at least when bluffing wasn't necessary. My old roommate had said I had an unfair advantage, since I spent my days doing advanced math calculations and had figured out how to count cards. I couldn't say he was entirely wrong, either.

When Sarah's mother pulled out a cribbage board I rubbed my hands together. I hadn't had fun with cards in half an eon. I had to bless Sarah's little gift to me, more than once, as the night advanced. She and her mother were more than competitive in the game, so we were all laughing when we were racing to 121 within a handful of points of each other.

Clark poked his head around the corner at the sounds of hilarity and joined us in a four-handed round, after I took the first one. So it ended up quite late before the fun was over, and we had successfully sidestepped all of the wedding planning details. I suspected Margaret had been in on the game, because she teased as she shepherded us up the stairs to our rooms. "Well. We missed out on the seating chart. I suppose we'll have to have you over tomorrow night."

I pretended contrition. "I'm sorry to put you through the trouble. I'm sure whatever you and Sarah have worked out is fine."

She flapped her hand at me. "You naughty boy. You're supposed to be involved in these details. After all, I don't know whether your

Aunt Mabel can even stand to sit at the same table as your Uncle Vern."

I was almost stupid enough to walk into that opening with a blurted "I wouldn't know either" but Sarah had caught a glimpse of my face and missed a step. I caught her with a muffled "oof" and then didn't bother to answer Margaret. We all fluttered around Sarah, and I apologized. "I'm sorry. I didn't realize just how late it was, and now Sarah's so tired she's stumbling. Let's get her settled first."

Margaret didn't miss my stratagem, and called for Hester again. The servant materialized at the head of the staircase. She took charge of me and led me down a hallway to an elegantly outfitted suite. Apparently I had stayed here before (or my things were being moved in ahead of the ceremony), because there were comfortable pajamas and a toothbrush waiting for me. I hoped Sarah would be able to sort out a clandestine visit in the night, despite the staff and parents in the house.

Hester knocked to take away my clothes for laundering and I had to remind myself that with these unknown patterns of activity it could be quite dangerous for us to have any unapproved dalliance— though it did seem that there was a bit of a conspiracy for us to have time together and it wouldn't be entirely cause for cursing were we to be caught in flagrante delicto.

I climbed into in the comfortable bed. It wasn't long before I was fighting sleep: I was well-fed, warm, in a human body, and a standard human house—bliss. It was an alluring recollection of my previous life and I wanted to savor every moment. Still, I fell asleep before Sarah managed to sneak in.

I was awoken by cold feet against my shins. Not the most enticing invitation I'd ever received, and it made me grumpy—until I realized that Sarah was just in a nightgown.

The night was cold and Sarah snuggled up to me. I did my best to warm her up. We were hungry for each other, but the possibility of being caught meant our kisses were tentative. We tried to be content to hold each other close and cherish this form of togetherness.

Eventually, my body reacted to her nearness. We were entangled in the sheets of a comfortable bed and it had been an untold age since last we had been together as humans. My fingertips stroked the unfamiliar frame of Sarah's new body. It was alluring: how many men dream of a variety of partners? Me? I had always been content with Sarah, but I had to admit having the chance to discover the new sensitive spots and erogenous zones titillated me. We were soon panting, all thoughts of potential interruptions shoved out of our heads by the joy of being together.

Chapter 27

At this point, I had come to assume that all our shifts would wait for several months before shoving us to our follow-on positions, so, as I was baring Sarah's thighs, and not thinking about much of anything, I ignored the tingles in my hands and feet as mere symptoms of the lust coursing through my body. Even the sparkles tingeing the edge of my vision seemed just part of the heated atmosphere we had created under the covers.

And then I was not in bed. I was standing in the middle of a busy sidewalk on a warm, late-spring day wearing shorts. My arousal hadn't had time to abate and my clothes didn't leave a lot to the imagination. I was mortified—the kind of feeling that will quickly enough douse the flames of desire. Not quickly enough that I didn't see a few smirks, or hear a few muffled gasps, as I tried to claim this body as my own. I had no idea where I was—other than it seemed to be a park, and I was apparently dressed for leisure.

When I finished blushing it was time to find a landmark. Where was I? It could have been a well-tended park anywhere in the western hemisphere. There were groomed and graveled pathways with deciduous trees strategically placed. Picnic blankets dotted the large stretches of trimmed grassland where families were enjoying the sun.

Given my discombobulation at the abrupt shift of venue, I couldn't even tell which way I had been headed when I entered this body, so I didn't know if I were on my way to or from someone. I sincerely hoped that Sarah was somewhere in this park with a picnic for the two of us.

I was thrilled to see I had hopped back into a human body. A surreptitious check of my hands showed me the standard five fingers in their anticipated positions.

There was a bench not too far off the walk. I walked over and sat. It was time to see if I could connect with the cellular memories of this form. I regretted that Sarah and I had been so involved with our physical needs that she never had managed to share the secret of her quick acclimation to a new form. If I could absorb the sun, and find my ease in this body, it might help me to find my footing, and regain the bearings I had lost in transition.

I was glad the bench was unoccupied. It wouldn't do to be the man who drove others off with his strange mutterings, because I thought talking to myself might help keep me focused on the task at hand.

Most of these transitions, as unanticipated as they might have been, had been easy on me. I took my cue from the picnickers by stretching out my legs, closing my eyes, and pretending I was absorbed in simple creaturely pleasures.

In reality, my mind was gyrating all over the map. Landing like this, where nobody was talking to me, or looking for me, or otherwise interacting with me, as anything other than a somewhat oddball, distracted person, made me empathize with those random tales of amnesia. I had no idea who I was supposed to be. If I couldn't figure out how to get to my home here, I might have to turn myself in to whatever variety of authority was available.

At that moment, I heard a strange whirring noise overhead, and re-opened my eyes to the world. In the distance I could see a dirigible overhead. At least there was evidence of some form of technology here. Maybe I was even still a scientist; I had never figured out in the previous body what I was supposed to have been. It was odd to have been sitting in on a sociology class, when that had historically been far outside my range of interests. Maybe it had been a strata-gem to impress Sarah's parents. Maybe I was more different in these new variations of worlds. I didn't know what to make of the situa-tion.

Sitting still, I noticed that the park visitors were all reacting in subtle ways to the overhead machine. Maybe it was more inimical than I had thought. Maybe I didn't want to be a scientist here, if this was the way our tools were greeted by the population.

Mothers were shepherding their children off the paths and to the scant protection under newly leafed trees. What was happening? Should I head for a tree too?

With fewer people strolling the walkways, I could see further. A lone female figure hurried in my direction. I sat up. Was it Sarah? I wouldn't know until I looked in her eyes, but the determination in her stride certainly boded well. I put the zeppelin out of mind and stood and shielded my eyes against the sun's glare. When she was 30 feet away, I decided that was indeed my Sarah.

She looked nothing like she had in any past body, with muscular arms and legs, and cropped hair. She was in a summer-weight uniform that reminded me of some sort of military branch back home. That was unusual for Sarah's inclinations, but the person looking out from behind those eyes was indubitably my girl. When I reached for her she hissed at me to put my hands down.

Sotto voce, she murmured, "I'm supposed to be here to take you into custody, so let's not confuse anyone by acting like ourselves."

I wobbled my head in confused acquiescence and fell in beside her. I finally had a chance to ask, "How is it that you find out these things so quickly every time we shift?"

She hid a quick grin and gestured discretely toward her ear. Now I could see the little bud tucked into her ear canal. I was distracted by the beautiful auburn shade of her hair; it looked a lot like what she had worn at home, and it was all I could do not to reach out and touch it.

She made another small gesture, and I could see she was pointing to a walkie-talkie-like device that was emitting static noises faintly in the background. She murmured again. "Not sure how much the boys upstairs can understand of what I whisper, but I think we need to keep conversation and contact to a minimum."

Eerily, the small device emitted a squawk just after she finished her statement and we both heard, "Inman? Come in."

She unclipped the radio from her belt and lifted it to her mouth. "Yes, sir? Over."

"Confirm apprehension of Dr. Inman. Over."

She eyed me speculatively. "Confirmed. Over."

"Proceed to the landing field for transport. Over."

"Confirmed. Over and out."

She had the military patter down pat. She turned down the volume on the radio, and motioned me forward. She unplugged the earpiece and let it dangle down the front of her uniform. She seemed distraught. I figured if I were recognized with the "doctor" appellation here, I had a good chance of being given access to what we would need to get home, but the look in Sarah's eyes made me wonder whether that would be possible. Apprehension and transport certainly didn't sound inviting.

Sarah took a deep, settling breath, and in a quick sibilance of words, rushed to whisper, "Mark... I can't let them take you into custody. We're married here too, and they want me to prove my loyalty to the state by turning you over to one of the research branches. But their security and systems make what we lived a few hops back look like child's play. I would never see you again—you would be part of a military machine working on top-secret weapons. And I know you: you would hate yourself for being cornered into that work, and you would hate me for putting you in that position. I would be nothing more than an intermittent bonus for you whenever they decided you needed a pat on the back. I couldn't take conjugal visits for the sole purpose of rewarding your work! Make it look like you overpowered me and run!"

I was stunned at this impassioned speech. Sarah had always supported me and my goals—it was one of the things I loved about her. But to hear her push me away to make sure I wouldn't have to work on warheads was overwhelming.

She started hitting me. I guess it was part of her act to make my escape look good, but in this body, her assault packed a punch. I didn't want to react. I wanted to be with Sarah however I could get her. I couldn't believe she was actually putting some force behind her fists in an effort to get me to respond. I was going to end up with bruises, and I still couldn't bring myself to retaliate. I didn't care if I got ribbed for being beaten up by a woman who was smaller than me. I needed Sarah to know that I was fine with doing what it took to be with her.

It was her sobbing that undid me. I never knew how to respond the right way to her tears. But when I would have gathered her into my arms to try to soothe her, she redoubled her efforts at pounding me into a pulp. In the end, our one-sided fight went on long enough that soldiers from her platoon found us and carried me away. Her effort had been for naught. And while I suspected she was going to gain kudos for so thoroughly putting me in my place, I could see the self-loathing upon her face.

That was the worst part of this dimensional shifting. While we were always ourselves, and knew ourselves from our origins, we were being placed in positions where we were being forced to operate against our own interests. While I was not as elastic as Sarah in understanding the cellular memories we would inherit from each new body, I was a lot more adaptive in finding ways to continue to pursue my ultimate goal—getting both of us back home.

As I was trussed hand and foot and shuffled on board the landed airship, I could see why the local population mistrusted the vehicle. There was an entire platoon housed in the chamber below the oversized balloon, and they had spread out around the base of the vehicle to clear the field of any civilians to ensure that nobody interfered with my incarceration.

I was dumped unceremoniously into a small, barred cell, alone in the center of the dirigible's main housing. The soldiers all filed in to take up posts around the inner perimeter. I was a goldfish on display in a bowl.

Sarah was taken to a different portion of the housing, I suspected so she could pull herself together for her debriefing. I felt utterly frustrated by how brief our interaction had been.

All I knew was that I had achieved an advanced degree, and the government wanted me to work on some kind of weaponry. What kind of society was this, where Sarah and I were married, but were going to be kept apart?

Getting upset was not going to help us, so I considered why it was that this latest bounce had come so quickly on the heels of the previous one. I hadn't been in the previous body a whole day. Thankfully I had jumped into a human body and was headed toward some real technology.

Was there a chance Sarah and I had caused the faster shift when we raised our energy while being non-corporeal? Maybe, if I were to start hyperventilating now, I could induce a shift. Would both of us need to do that at the same time to be more effective? I wished some of the psi gifts we had had in earlier form had translated with us.

Come to think of it, I had never tested whether they might not have. After all, my Sarah had been with me all along; she would have had as good a chance at that talent transference as I would. More telling, she was the one who was finding it so easy to adapt to life in these other bodies. Maybe she had figured out how to carry forward some of those mind-reading skills and that was how she was fitting in so easily and discovering so much about the different worlds around us.

I decided this was worth a test. So I ignored all the stares and closed my eyes, settling down on the bare floor of my cell to do my best impression of a yogi. Five minutes in and I felt my butt and legs going to sleep. Even if I wasn't on the right track, this was a good way of ignoring the discomfort of the vast unknown yawning before me. To mitigate my circulatory issues, I stretched out on the floor. It seemed clean and it was quiet enough that I could have fallen asleep, had the tension level around me gone down a notch or two.

That thought startled me. Maybe composing myself this way was opening up my access to those psi talents after all. Normally, I wouldn't have noticed the emotional atmosphere. I was generally too wrapped up in my trials to pay much attention to anything other than my results, and had been accused, more than once, of being obtuse. Sarah had been the only one to reach past that single-minded focus with ease. Maybe she had already had some psi skills before we bounced into those bodies, and that was part of her advantage in accessing them throughout our travels.

I took another deep breath. If I focused on the emotional tension, I could start feeling my way toward Sarah and try to coordinate my hyperventilation test with her. Another deep breath. I thought I could feel her reaching toward me too. I tried to frame the suggestion to her, imagining the picture of the two of us huffing and puffing. I could feel my breath quicken and deepen. I hoped Sarah was working with me on this.

In the end, my lungs were inflating and deflating like a bellows. I would take what followed as all the evidence I needed that in this, as in everything else, Sarah was fully committed to what I was pursuing. My hands and feet started tingling. I inhaled more deeply and let the breath whistle out of my lungs with speed and force. Stars peppered my vision. This was working. I was vaguely aware of booted feet rushing toward my cell. I didn't care. I was going to bring on another switch, and Sarah and I were going to be out of this disaster.

Chapter 28

When I looked up next, I was on a wooden sidewalk beside a cobblestone road. I was holding Sarah by the shoulders and looking at a face that was drawn and malnourished. I needed to make sure she knew I loved her, but the tingles in my hands and feet were not slowing down. I tried to hold on tighter and knew I scared her with the force in my hands. She slipped away from me and dashed down the street to a storefront with a milliner's sign hanging over the window.

I planned to chase after her, but couldn't coordinate my movements. I didn't know why, if she were my Sarah, she would be running from me. We had always run toward each other before. Was she ashamed of how she had treated me in bringing me to the authorities? I didn't care. She had done it out of love, trying to save me from the obligation to work on projects she knew I wouldn't want to work on.

The tingles still weren't slowing down, and now the sparkles were encroaching on the edge of my vision. I wondered if we had made a mistake in forcing a shift while we were in uncomfortable circumstances. Certainly, we didn't seem much better off here than the last version of the world—aside from the fact that we were no longer on opposite sides of the law. I tried one final time to get my breathing under control, but the next time I looked up, the scene had shifted again.

This was happening too quickly. If I couldn't slow down the shifts, how would I ever run the trials necessary to get us back home? I held my breath. This would eventually make me feel tingly, and would make me black out too, but maybe that would stop the dimensions from spinning wildly around me.

My heart was still pounding when I opened my eyes to a tranquil forest scene. This setting would do a lot to temper my racing pulse. All I had to do was focus. Musical birdsong, gentle breeze, sunlight filtering through the new leaves on the trees; it was a perfect place to escape from an overwrought mind. If I could just stay here long enough to let it settle into my bones.

Standing there, looking at the undersides of the leaves, I was reminded me of the park where Sarah had found me. Thinking of her in military gear caused my pulse to race again. This was not good. If I couldn't control this new gallop through space-time, we might never be tethered again.

I forced my breath to stillness again. At least I was in human form. It felt much more natural to be holding my breath when I knew how my lungs worked.

I heard shuffling through the underbrush. Adrenalin coursed through my system. I spun around and was rewarded with a fleeting view of a startled deer. That's what I must look like to anyone who might be watching me. I was infecting myself with paranoia. But at least I had been here a few minutes longer than I had on that street in the turn-of-the-century-looking wherever it had been.

I folded my hands together and bowed my head. I'd never prayed before, but it looked like a peaceful pose. Maybe it would help me collect myself. Was Sarah close? I liked that we were more regularly in human bodies now, despite the fact that we had been able to spend more time together when we were in alternate forms. Was that an evil conspiracy against us by those messengers who had been so kind to point out the obvious? There was no way of knowing. Besides, that was crediting us with more significance than we deserved, being but two human souls, lost on our path through life.

Now that I was paying more attention, and able to stay focused on the view around me, I noticed it wasn't quite as wild as the passing deer might have indicated. The grass beneath my feet was short, and I could see another groomed path not too far in the distance. I had to talk sternly to my pulse, not to have some kind of PTSD attack—since that was where things had gone so wrong with Sarah. My reluctant feet took halting steps toward the path. Once there, I saw the area was deserted. I guess that would account for the birds being calm enough to continue singing. I stood still and sniffed the air. A fragrance reminiscent of Sarah's beef stew reached my nose and my stomach grumbled. Checking the angle of the sun and my shadow, I figured it to be about 4pm. My stomach won, and I continued along the path, toward what I hoped was dinner.

Before I walked too far I looked down to survey my body and clothes to make sure I wouldn't scare anyone off by appearing as a vagabond. I was respectably dressed in slacks, a shirt, and a sweater vest. This was strange attire for walking through the woods, so maybe I had been invited to a private party.

Remembering Sarah's skill with the psi levels of communication, I chose to calm my breathing even more, to see whether I could reach out to her. Maybe if she could hear my calmness and rationality, she wouldn't skitter away from me. I hoped, anyway. I leaned against a tall tree nearer the path, the better to focus on what I had to do. This time, I ignored the shuffling when it came again.

In fact, there was something strangely familiar about these woods. I remembered having chosen a cabin not too far from the Alaskan installation as our honeymoon destination. We were going to retreat from society and live like hermits for two weeks to celebrate our nuptials. Sarah and I had talked about how we were going to stock the cabin. We had planned our meals so we wouldn't have to leave. There were lots of soups, and eggs, and noodles, and rice on our proposed menu.

A wave of nostalgia washed over me. What I wouldn't give to have made it back before our wedding night. Not to have run that blasted trial. I didn't even care about the Higgs particle at this point. I just wanted my life back—my life with Sarah. We had tasted what it would be like to have children, raise them, love them, and feel like a family together. It wouldn't be fair if we couldn't do that in the original setting where we had started that course of action.

I took another settling breath. When I opened my eyes I just stared, then rubbed my eyes to make sure. There was Sarah, standing shyly in front of me. She was a little daintier than I remembered, but then, I had just seen her muscled up as a soldier, so maybe she had always been that petite. She held her hand out to me. It was the only invitation I needed to rush toward her. She had tears in her eyes again, but this time she huddled against me as I held her.

She shuddered with quiet sobs and finally managed to say: "I think we're home. This smells like Alaska to me. And that cabin further up the path looks just like the one we planned to honeymoon in. It's even stocked with the food we had planned to bring with us. I recognize the clothes in the closet."

I stared at her in wonder. After that much time and worry and effort, all it had taken was coordinated breathing to get the two of us home? It seemed too good to be true. I wasn't going to look a gift horse in the mouth. I looped my arm around Sarah's shoulder and asked, "Is it too late to carry you over the threshold for the first time?"

She giggled and slung her arms around my neck. I lifted her up and carried her into the cabin. The calendar on the wall was set for June 2012. It was surreal to be home again—and with so little effort on my part. The question, though, was: could we stay now that we had made it this far?

A voracious reader since she was a toddler, and an ordained spiritu-
alist, Tonya Cannariato has now presided over the marriage of her
love of reading and her love of writing. She's lived a nomadic life,
following first her parents in their Foreign Service career through
Africa, Europe, and Asia, and then her own nose criss-crossing
America as she's gotten old enough to make those choices for
herself. She's currently based in the Washington, DC area with her
four loves: her husband and three Siberian Huskies. She suspects
her Huskies of mystical alchemy with their joyous liberation of her
muse and other magical beings for her inspiration. She loves to
sleep, to watch her interesting dreams, some of which are now finding new life in
written form.

If you're interested in news & future releases, you can find her
online at http://www.facebook.com/TonyaCannariato, Twitter
@tmycann, or her author website at http://tmycann.com.

Thank you for purchasing *Dementional*. You can claim a free copy of the eBook version by going to http://katarrkanticlespress.com/ and clicking on 'Claim Your Free Ebook Copy'. Please read the information on that page before logging in.

The login information is as follows:

Username: Dementional

Password: BJi2Korw

Other Novels By This Author

Dust to Blood (Red Slaves #1)

Blood to Fire (Red Slaves #2)

Other Titles From Katarr Kanticles Press

Arcane Solutions (Discord Jones #1)

Crooked Fang

Indigo Dancer

After the Fall: Far From Home

After the Fall: A Warrior's Worth

www.ingramcontent.com/pod-product-compliance
Lightning Source LLC
Chambersburg PA
CBHW060148130626
46556CB00006B/2553